IRA LIPMA 1973

JUNE @

BOT NEW YORK NY

NOTHING BUT THE BEST

Nothing but the Best

The Luck of the Jewish Princess

Leslie Tonner

Coward, McCann & Geoghegan

New York

*To **Robert**, for everything*

CONTENTS

PREFACE

When I was twelve years old, living in the heart of a gilded ghetto on Long Island known as the Five Towns, a group of girls in my school decided to form a club. They were the ritziest clique in the class; before I and the backward, unchic few had given up our white socks and sneakers, they had nylon stockings and panty girdles. And when they unveiled their new organization, they did it in high style.

One morning, like so many young birds of paradise, they paraded into school en masse sporting their brand-new shiny blue snap jackets with reversible black linings. Stitched on the front, over the heart, their first names: Louise, Sandra, Adrian, Pamela. And on the back, in languid black script, the club name, The Ideals.

Now that takes chutzpah. To think that at the age of twelve you can assume you're everyone's ideal! But did these girls have any second thoughts? Of course not. They merely went on through the eighth grade cracking their chewing gum between their teeth and wearing their shiny, Ideal blue through rain and snow.

Preface

All were Jewish Princesses, bursting into adolescent bloom, who would have their teeth straightened, their noses fixed, their hair streaked so that they could arrive in a blaze of thirteen-year-old glory at the Copacabana on prom night, limp orchids pinned to the top of their gold lamé and net dresses.

Most young girls at ninety-eight percent Jewish P.S. 6 in Woodmere were princesses, daughters of parents who moved to the suburbs to offer their children better lives. And what lives they were, filled with the rites of puberty in princessland: invitations to dozens of choice bar mitzvahs (and to be the bar mitzvah boy's date for the party was the place of honor), summers away at Vermont and Pennsylvania camps, piano lessons on the baby grand, strings of pearls and gold bangle bracelets for birthday gifts, ballroom dancing classes to learn the cha-cha, fox-trot and lindy, and encouragement to achieve in school, rack up grade points, intelligence test scores and proper extra curricular activities lists so as to gain admittance to the "right" colleges. In four years would follow marriage to a nice Jewish premedical, dental or law student and the cycle would be complete.

When I started research for this book, I knew about the princesses of Long Island and New York. What I did not realize was that wherever Jewish families settled in America, there were Jewish Princesses. They lived not only in other gilded ghettos (Short Hills, Shaker Heights, Beverly Hills), but also in cities I had never associated before with Jewish anything: Seattle, Kansas City (Missouri), Minneapolis–St. Paul, Phoenix. A friend of mine who spent a year traveling throughout the country (and eating

x

only kosher food—it's a miracle he found enough to survive) said that no matter how small and isolated a town, "if there's a Kleinfeld's Department Store and Mr. Kleinfeld has a daughter, there's a Jewish Princess around somewhere."

And as I interviewed Jewish Princesses, Princes and their families for this book, I began to see that when people used the phrase "Jewish Princess" they meant all those things I had felt about The Ideals: "Princess" had the connotation of "spoiled, pampered, overbearing, snotty, materialistic." But the more I met the real thing, the more I came to see their strengths, their intelligence and their marvelous ability to laugh at themselves, and with these more positive views, my own background became more relevant. I too had adoring parents who provided me with orthodontia, camp, music and dancing lessons, and like many of the young women described in these pages, I came out of this environment rather well equipped to stand up for myself, to work hard and to believe in my abilities. These are the attitudes that now seem to me to be more of a common denominator for Jewish Princesses than clothing labels, credit cards, interior decorators or number of days per week you have a maid.

But in addition to exploring the princess' strengths, I could not ignore the funny side of being raised female and Jewish, the rites of becoming a Princess. Being Jewish is different, and being raised as a Jewish daughter in America is a very special proposition. I decided to spell out the borders of her world as well.

Everything and everyone mentioned in this book are

real. The celebrities are undisguised, but the nonfamous are for the most part given different names and occupations according to their wishes. The young women refused to acknowledge publicly that they might be princesses, and the men were afraid their wives and/or girl friends might detect some anti-princess bias. I hope this book may help change a few negative attitudes.

Finally, a few people deserve thanks for their help. A proper Jewish Princess would write a little note on Tiffany paper, monogrammed with her initials. I haven't any such stationery, so the thank-you will be public, to my parents for support, encouragement and love to Peggy Brooks, my editor, for helpful comments and suggestions, to the famous and not-so-famous Jewish Princesses and Princes whose warmth and cooperation made working on this book a pleasure, and most of all, much gratitude and I-couldn't-have-done-it-without-you to Joan Raines, my agent.

NOTHING BUT THE BEST

1

THE DAUGHTER ALSO RISES

> If I could come back reincarnated as anything
> in the world, I'd want to be a Jewish granddaughter.
> —A Jewish grandfather, ca. 1974

In the springtime of student upheavals in 1968, when middle-class masses at many colleges and universities rose up to challenge the Establishment, there was a great awakening at Columbia University. Everyone who read the papers or watched the news on television was familiar with the scenes of turmoil. News film footage showed giant buildings taken over by groups of newly radicalized young men and women waving banners and clenched fists. Photographs went out on the wire services picturing the college president's office where students smoked cigars, propped their feet up on the hitherto sacred desk and flipped through confidential files and papers. The city of New York sent scores of riot police to the campus where they cordoned off the embattled inner zone. A ring of student pickets and sympathizers marched daily around the school, shouting slogans, skirmishing with onlookers and with the weary police. Marching along Broadway just

15

outside the great metal gates to the campus were two young men, Marshall and Larry. They carried signs, "Columbia Trustees are Racist Pigs," "Up Against the Wall, Grayson Kirk." They watched with interest the comings and goings of police, the arrests and general mayhem. Suddenly Larry spotted a Barnard girl he knew emerging from a yellow taxi, banner in hand, clad in tight, washed-out jeans and a suede jacket. He turned to his friend Marshall and pointed her out. "That's a real Jewish Princess," Larry said. "When the revolution comes, she arrives in a cab."

That Barnard girl, with her college education, her involvement with world events, and her chic battle dress, represents an extraordinary 180-degree shift in the status of the Jewish daughter. Had that girl been born during the past two thousand years of Jewish life in the Old World, the odds were high she would have been a Jewish peasant, a household drudge regarded as a burden by her family. Parental responsibilities toward her were to see that she was married off as soon as possible. Today, after a mere seven or eight decades in America, Jewish daughters are called Jewish Princesses. They are cultivated, educated, cultured, valuable investments.

Only after the Jews arrived in America did a transformation in the daughter's role take place. And it was an unexpected metamorphosis. They came to the New World dreaming of great advances for their sons. But no one anticipated what affect the combination of Jewish traditions and American striving would have on the dark-eyed, solemn little daughter.

In America, the daughter's life did not come to include

some practices that formerly kept her in a secondary position: the mikva (ritual bath), the dowry, the arranged match, the sheytl (wig). But she did benefit from a retention of the Jewish family's child-centered orientation. Thus, traditional Jewish love, encouragement, nagging, pushing and swooning over a child joined hands with the thrust for upward mobility to produce the Jewish American Princess. She is in part the shtetl daughter ("You should marry well. Such a good match will bring us great naches [joy]."). But she is an American, expected to achieve, to Do Well ("What do you mean you only got ninety-eight on that science test? Who got the hundred?"). And she is a princess by virtue of her specialness to her parents ("Harry, look at that pitcher she made in ceramics! Did you ever see such talent?").

There is a history behind the Jewish Princess, an old, familiar story to be sure, but one which must be told in order to know from whence the Jewish Princess came. Just prior to immigration, the life of a Jewish daughter was about as glamorous as a kreplach, that humble, homemade dumpling which floats in soup. Kreplach is a very unsexy, substantial food. The Jewish daughter was much the same; trained under her mother's wing, she learned the ins and outs of keeping kosher, to cook, clean, sew, market, scrub, polish and run a proper Jewish home. Any education she received was desultory at best, in Yiddish for the most part. Instruction in Hebrew was reserved for men; women did not study Torah and Talmud. Sons brought respect and blessings to a family through a life of study; daughters brought problems, chief among them the necessity of a dowry.

Once in America, the golden, promised land, parents began a brand-new business: improving a daughter's life. Jewish boys traditionally followed their own upwardly mobile path (hard work, study, learning to become rabbis in the old country transformed into becoming doctors, lawyers, professionals in the new land). But who knew what to do with a daughter? The only specific plans anyone could recall were to marry her off, fast. So in America, a new way to raise daughters took root in the immigrants' desire to Take Advantage of Everything, particularly WASP propriety. They would give her not only good schools but also fine clothes, music and dancing lessons, culture, all of the correct finishing touches.

The real key to the Jewish Princess is found in the change in parents' attitudes. No change was more important or revolutionary than in what they expected for their little girls. Emma Goldberg (an Ellis Island stand-in for Grushenik) and her husband believed that they could improve their daughters' lives. The Goldbergs, arriving in America at the turn of the century with little money and ten children, took advantage of new opportunities immediately. By following the lives of the Goldberg females through several generations in this country, the rise of the daughter can be charted.

What did America have to offer the little Jewish girl? Free education, to start. Late at night, Emma stitched new first-day-at-school outfits for her sons and daughters. "All my children will have time to study. A real mitsva, a true blessing, thank God," Emma said. Emma, her hair pinned into a tight bun, dressed in a fringed shawl and long skirt, would lead a life remarkably similar to her shtetl existence, as caretaker for her large family. "But my daughters, they will not have to work so hard," Emma thought. "For them it will be different, a better life."

The contrast between immigrant Emma and her youngest daughter, Rebecca, was stunning. The mother appeared stocky, firm, rooted to the earth with lined, worn face and rough hands. Rebecca, born just before the move to America, was a New World child. A photograph of her at age ten shows her hair tied back with a ribbon off a soft face. She does not look as though she works in the kitchen. Instead, she is dressed up, shiny and neat, in a starchy, handsewn, long dress.

Life was indeed better for Rebecca than it was for her mother. By the time Becky was thirteen, she had completed seven years of school and in her closet were handmade, neatly pressed outfits and a new pair of shoes. Her brothers would even go to college. The eldest was at City College already, preparing for dental school. Then the crisis fell. Becky's father died and she had to leave school along with the other daughters to work as a seamstress. Becky worked until 1916 when, at twenty, she married a man in the textile business. But during those seven years of work, Becky had accumulated dreams. She vowed that her children would finish high school and college and have all the things her own parents wanted for her but could not afford.

Thus the first generation of Jewish Princesses was born at the moment in time when Jewish expectation first met the American Dream. These princesses seem humble by today's standards but deserve the title because they belonged to the first generation who fulfilled their parents' hopes.

Rebecca's daughter Esther took on more of the characteristics we associate with the term "Jewish Princess." Born in 1920, the year her parents moved out of the ghetto and into a better neighborhood, Esther was a little girl with shiny, clipped hair, a big white bow resting on top of her head, so big it was almost the size of a hat, high white stockings and a blue and white sailor dress. After school, eight-year-old Esther skipped home along the tree-lined, neatly tended streets of Brooklyn, clutching a paper she wrote on Christopher Columbus that earned her two gold stars. "Two stars," she told her mother. "Nobody else got more than one!" Esther knew this was right up her mother's alley. "See?" said Momma. "I always told you your work was the best. Now, you know what else you have to work on." Obedient Esther nodded and pushed open the door to the tiny cramped front room, the family parlor. Inside that small space, next to the couch with its plumped-up pillows and antimacassars, and hard by the polished, gleaming wood sideboard with its set of worn religious texts (Esther always thought God lived there), was the real symbol of advancement to Rebecca. The mahogany ivoried piano, in shining splendor. The Steinway, first concrete symbol of scrimping and saving and doing something measurably better for your child. Esther, unaware of what the piano represented, only knew she had to practice. Climbing up onto the piano bench, she began her scales.

The piano and music lessons were silently understood by Momma and Poppa to be Jewish Princess territory. But as the sounds of the dogged piano practice filtered through the little apartment, Becky's son Abel wandered into the kitchen. He watched his mother drop pennies into her pushkes, the little tin containers lined up on the window ledge that held money for charities, for the Jewish homeland and for household expenses. "What's that one for?" he asked as she picked up an unlabeled tin. "For Esther's piano lessons," Momma answered. "Why can't I have music too?" Abel pressed on. "Because," his mother answered, "you have cheder [Hebrew school] every day, don't you? This other box is for your lessons. Your sister will learn to play the piano and you will be a rabbi."

The precious boy, Momma and Poppa's little Kaddish, found his place as star sapphire in the family usurped by this little girl, playing a mangled version of "Für Elise" in the other room. Certainly Esther was a Jewish Princess by very modest standards indeed, but she was able to finish high school, even attend Hunter College, have music lessons and an occasional summer trip *en famille* to a little house in the Rockaways. By comparison with her mother, she was some kind of princess. Still, her clothes, though immaculate, were homemade, Hunter was a free, public school, and Edgemere was not a fancy summer camp in the Berkshires. But Abel says he remembers a trip Esther made with his mother one summer to a Catskills hotel when Esther was twenty. "Mother sewed and ironed and cleaned and brushed everything, and wrapped it in tissue, carefully, a whole trunk full of clothes. Esther went away like a princess!" A modest beginning, but a start all the same.

On one of those Catskills forays, Esther snared a young doctor ("Kineahorah," said Momma and Poppa), and by 1944, when her husband went overseas, had a two-year-old daughter. After the war, they moved into an apartment on Central Park West. ("Fancy," said Momma with great pride.) Like many other Jewish families who had made some kind of financial arrival into the middle class by the 1940's, Esther and her husband were prepared to give their daughter everything. The quickest look at exactly what "everything" meant is to walk into their apartment, intact and identical to this day. In the living room, long, carpeted wall-to-wall, are a nicely upholstered set of matching couch and club chairs, the inherited piano, fine china ashtrays and matching cigarette box (Wedgwood), two built-in areas for books, the popular classics, *Exodus, Gone with the Wind,* a set of Winston Churchill's World War II series, a sprinkling of Daphne du Maurier and Edna Ferber. Over the couch, with a small brass light attached to the top, cord running down, is a full-color, soft-toned portrait of daughter Susan at age ten. Susan sits in a background of pastel, powder blue tones, pretty, almost beautiful, in a smocked, pleated, pale yellow dress with short puffed sleeves and a tiny round white collar, a Lord & Taylor classic. On her wrist is a little gold bracelet. Her hands are folded in her lap, and she is leaning forward slightly. Brown hair is combed and styled, turned toward her face, the hair held off her forehead by a tiny barrette. She is smiling slightly, lips turned up but folded over her teeth to cover her extensive orthodontia.

The Daughter Also Rises

Portrait of a Jewish Princess. Susan at age ten was a veteran of two summers at Camp Weeloncken, where she learned tennis, horseback riding, swimming, and, during rest hour, how to set her hair and apply nail polish. (No nail polish is evident in the portrait; her mother had not known about that skill yet.) On the piano are tattered remnants of her music lessons, classical piano, "Easy Themes You Love to Play" and, later on, simplified Rachmaninoff for a small recital. With Susan's intelligence attested to by nursery school and kindergarten teachers who gave IQ tests early in her progressive schools, Susan attended Riverdale, an expensive, excellent, private day school in a green-wooded, demi-suburb of Manhattan.

More than anything else in that living room, the portrait of Susan, and her life at age ten, represented her family's real arrival in the middle to upper middle class. The act of hiring a portrait painter to come and reproduce the little daughter, rather than portraits of the parents to be revered by the children, indicated how special that daughter was and what it meant to her parents every time they looked at her painted image hanging over their couch. Of course their son, who became a doctor (what else?) brought them great pride and joy but the little girl, seated in clouds of pastel blue, was the delight and the center of attention, love and activity, and they could not do enough for her.

Susan has her own little girl now, Jennifer, nine years old. They live in a very expensive house in Scarsdale, New York, an upper-middle-class suburb known for its well-to-do populace. Susan's husband is a lawyer, but at thirty-four he really can't afford the lavishly decorated house, the golf club, the two cars, as easily as expected. But not to worry, the couple is being shtupped by Susan's parents. (In Yiddish, shtup means to push upward, and vulgarly, to fornicate, but among the Jewish American middle class it has yet another meaning: parents laying a lot of financial help on their married young.)

Three generations of Jewish women play out the familiar scenario of doing things for the children. Grandma Esther believes "Susan and Jennifer must have as much as possible, the best of everything. I'll make sure they do." Grandma helped pay to decorate the house, and for Jennifer's pink tutu, leotards, ballet lessons, summer camp and jewelry (a small gold heart with a tiny ruby at its center and a little strand of pearls). Susan thinks, "This is the right way to raise a daughter. It's nice that my mother wants to do so much, but if she weren't giving Jennifer all those things, I'd be doing it myself. It's the right way to do things. It's always been that way, hasn't it?" And Jennifer? The necessary object of all this attention, she shrugs her shoulders. She's come to expect it. "Say 'thank you' to Grandma, Jennifer," Susan says. "Thank you, Grandma," Jennifer parrots.

During the summer of 1973, Susan, her husband, and her parents made their monthly trip to summer camp to visit Jennifer. They send her away from home but, somewhat guilty, feel it is necessary to bring home to Jennifer at least twice during an eight week summer. So after the weekly care packages and almost daily letters have been sent out for three weeks, the four were ready to take the long drive to Vermont. This particular summer it

24

was a tense trip. Jennifer, it seemed, did not want to go to camp. Home is more fun, she argued, "I can swim in the club pool and take tennis lessons. I don't understand why I have to go to camp." Susan, grim-faced, told her, "I just don't know why you don't like it. I loved camp. My summers were terrific." Grandma and Grandpa relaxed in the back of the Lincoln Continental. Jennifer's disloyalty was carefully hidden from them since they foot the bills. The Vermont camp was the third Jennifer attended in as many summers in an attempt to find the place which would meet with her approval. "Dear Mom and Dad," her last critical letter said, "there is a very mean councilor [sic] who made me pay for a horse bridle I broke. pleas send me more money, for some candy. Love, Jennifer. p.s. when you come up, pleas stay a week."

When they arrived at camp, they went to Jennifer's bunk. She appeared overly glad to see them and when asked if she liked this camp, said nothing. "Of course she likes it," Grandma said. "It's so beautiful, to be away for the summer from the heat, out in the country." Jennifer did not answer, but her grandmother's remark puzzled her. As far as Jennifer is concerned, she lives all year round in "the country" in Scarsdale, so what's the difference about camp? Just before visiting weekend was over, Jennifer told her parents she wanted to stay home next summer. "No," said Susan. "Absolutely not. We'll find you another camp." Driving home, the grandparents asleep in the back of the car, Susan turned to her husband. "She'll like camp if I have to send her to twenty. She's supposed to enjoy it, damn it!"

Once privileges of the princess, the accoutrements are now *de rigueur.* Think of how the ghetto child would have kvelled over a summer in camp, one which even featured a kosher kitchen, chopped liver and all. But Jewish parents are not content to offer their child mere tokens, the child must use them, otherwise there is no meaning in the giving, in making life better. Difficult as it is for a woman like Susan, who had so much, to make life measurably better for Jennifer, she still tries very hard. She has to see improvement. Jennifer must take advantage of camp, just as her great grandmother Rebecca took advantage of school, her grandmother Esther of music lessons, her mother Susan of private school and a posh women's college. The next generation? They won't even have to like camp. If they don't want to go, parents tell them, "Fine. We'll travel. Would you like to visit Israel?"

All of these advantages do not mean that a Jewish Princess comes out spoiled rotten. Many are high achievers, hard workers and much of their success has to do with their being first and foremost in their parents' eyes. The Jewish Princess can rise to heights of glory, as far from the shtetl as Rabbi Sally Priesand, the first ordained woman rabbi in Jewish history. Rabbi Priesand is now, at twenty-seven, one of those remarkable "firsts" who wishes everyone would get over marveling at her position and allow her to get on with her work. Confident and businesslike, she sits behind a large wooden desk in a spacious but slightly worn and unpretentious office at the Stephen Wise Free Synagogue on Manhattan's Upper West Side. No pampered, regal princess, she. Rabbi

Priesand is unroyally dressed in eyeglasses, plain blouse, simple wool skirt, with her long straight brown hair tucked behind her ears. The book-filled office, desk piled high with papers, appointment calendar clogged with business, underline her seriousness of purpose, her scholarly occupation. She is, after all, a rabbi. But then, too, she is bright, funny, and wryly amused at discussing Jewish Princesses. "Maybe I'm a little bit of one. I had my parents' support, always. Whatever they could do for me, for my two brothers and sister, they did, whatever we wanted. But they never asked me, 'What kind of job is this for a nice Jewish girl?' "

So, Rabbi Priesand, do you think that being a Jewish Princess is all that bad for a child? If it means rich, spoiled brat, it is, Rabbi Priesand says. But, the rabbi notes, Jewish children are treated as important members of the family. "If a kid makes a brilliant remark, maybe snotty, he's appreciated, he's encouraged. Overprotectiveness actually gives the Jewish child more time. The child can do what he chooses, study what he likes, without having to worry about taking care of himself. If the children need anything, they know their parents are there. A certain kind of nagging can also stimulate children to do better things." And, says Rabbi Priesand, just giving children material things does not instantaneously make them spoiled brats. "Jewish parents do things for their children because they think it's an advantage for them. The things are not a substitute for love."

Rabbi Priesand illustrates the point well. What she appreciates most about her childhood is not what her parents did for her materially, but their support and encouragement. Developing children in that fashion goes back to life on the shtetl, back to when Jewish parents told four- or five-year-old children, "Zay a mentsh" [Be a person]. In the golden land, America, the Jewish daughter was and is given every opportunity to be a fourteen-carat golden person for the first time in Jewish history. So naturally, she takes advantage. Who wouldn't?

It is likely the Jewish Princess would not be around at all were it not for the fortuitous marriage of Jewish culture and the "American way." The mating was an accident of fate, but its offspring have flourished. The Princess is an acknowledged success. But is she the neatly pigeonholed stereotype painted in broad strokes in comedy monologues, novels or movie scripts? In certain cases, the honest answer is yes. Everyone knows some girl or group of girls just like that media image, pampered, spoiled little darlings. But there are plenty of other Jewish Princesses who fail to fit one specific mold and who tempt me to throw out any previous definitions of the term. For argument's sake, the Jewish Princess will be defined as simply as possible: anyone born female and Jewish in America. Further description, details, embellishments, curlicues and the like will be provided by our New World Cinderella, the Jewish Princess herself.

2

GODDAMMIT, I CAN DO ANYTHING!

> Women are a nation by themselves.
> —The Talmud

Rumor has it that the real Jewish Princess is poured in plastic into a mold. There are women who resemble the assembly-line Jewish Princess as closely as their fake Gucci shoes with their gold chains and shiny heels match the originals ("I got these at Saks"). They jangle their gold bangles, toss their blown-dry Sassoon hairstyles, and march off down the street with their Lhasa apsos in tow, each little dog with a cunning hair ribbon or tortoiseshell barrette in its streaked doggie hair.

But not every Jewish Princess is a wealthy, bejeweled, Vuitton-toting lady with a shopping mania, a doctor-husband and a nose job. Her left hand isn't always weighed down by a diamond as big as the Concord; her right hand doesn't continually clutch a Bloomingdale's shopping bag stuffed with glorious status impulse purchases.

Being a Jewish Princess has to do with heritage and upbringing, not with profiles or department store demeanor. Jewish heritage means a little girl has been more often than not an adored, beloved, golden child. She exhibits an unmistakable confidence, an inbred belief in herself that comes from being the center of attention in the most child-centered of homes. Her drive, her special chutzpah, is the real mark of the Jewish Princess, not her resemblance to any predefined stereotype.

Ethel Scull, taxi magnate's wife, Fifth Avenue matron, rich lady who collects art, likely candidate for Jewish Princess of the Year, has fooled everyone. Fooled her husband, her mother, her father, her three sons, her friends, because she did not pop straight out of the mold and behave exactly like others of her generation and background.

"I'm redecorating," Ethel says as she she opens the door to her eleven-room Fifth Avenue apartment. Stepping into her home is a rude shock. The place is bare, walls stripped of all the fabulous Pop and Op and abstract art that made the Sculls famous. There's no furniture, no "objets" to inspect, just a large foyer, an enormous living room, empty except for a cloth-covered baby grand and taxi magnate husband Bob, watching TV from a leather easy chair.

"Come with me," Ethel says, and following her through the twists and turns of a long hallway, it's hard to see the Beautiful Person, society lady, Jewish Princess Ethel photographed in the fashion pages. Why isn't she in a Halston Ultrasuede pants suit or a slinky Stephen Burrows number or even a Missoni sweater and custom-made, hand-embroidered Levi's? And where's the status stuff, the jewelry, chic hairstyle, the expensive, custom-made eyelashes? Ethel could easily blend into any group of mothers at a suburban PTA meeting. She is small, slight and ramrod straight and stiff from a broken back suffered in a fall several years ago in Barbados. She does not look fifty (though she's at least that age, married thirty years ago while in college), with shoulder-length streaked blond hair and taut, clear skin. She's stylishly skinny but is dressed ordinarily in yellow slacks, printed blouse, simple gold wedding band.

Ethel Scull, née Redner, was born to be a Jewish Princess. She was raised in the Manhattan Jewish community of the 1920's, a world bounded by Central Park West, West End Avenue, Saks Fifth Avenue, and Schrafft's. Youngest in the family, Daddy's favorite baby daughter, Ethel was the sole blond-haired, brown-eyed child in a dark, Semitic family. "Ethel, the glamour girl," Mama swooned as her youngest grew into a princess fatale who dated the pick of the Jewish Princes. The family kvelled. Ethel did not. Bored by the mold, her assigned role, she plotted rebellion.

What's rebellion for a nice Jewish girl? First Ethel brought home a non-Jewish boy. Oy. Then she took a summer job as a model when she was eighteen. Oy vay. Jewish girls aren't supposed to model; models were blond gentiles of low moral character and easy repute, as Mrs. Redner knew. "I should have a daughter who works with such terrible people? Such mishigoss," Mrs. Redner mourned. But wait. Once Ethel marries, like her sister, she'll settle down. She'll get over it. Mr. Redner, traditional

31

Jewish papa, had only one traditional comment. "But she'll graduate first, or else."

Mom and Dad breathed easier at last when Ethel got engaged at twenty to Robert Scull, a nice Jewish boy who presented Ethel with her requisite diamond engagement ring. But engaged Ethel rebelled again, and decided to get herself a job as an artist in advertising. Off she went, diamond ring and all, to NBC for an interview. The personnel director spotted the rock and wanted to know when Miss Redner was getting married. Ethel, sorry she wore the ring at all, convinced the interviewer that her impending marriage would not interfere except for time off for the wedding. She got the job. Triumphant Ethel, bursting with pride, ran home to tell her future husband of her first victory. She never anticipated his reaction. Not only was Bob Scull against this job, but he told her in no uncertain terms that no wife of his was ever going to work.

Ethel Redner soon-to-be Scull, rebellious but at heart a good Jewish girl, did what she was told. She turned down the NBC offer and to this date has never held a salaried job. Ethel was raised to be obedient; her parents emigrated from Eastern Europe and were Old World strict about behavior: "Never answer back." Like other Jewish Princesses of her generation, Ethel would take care of her lovely husband and have beautiful children, whose arrival signaled Suburbs Time. "Never bring children into the dirty city," Mamma said, to which Bob added, "Right." Out to Great Neck went the Scull family. In the early 1950's Ethel traded her dream of a Manhattan town house for a spacious home on Long Island. The suburbs offered quiet, secure streets, wide lawns, gracious homes, two-car garages, good schools, country clubs, established synagogues, cards and Mah-Jongg. "I hated it," says Ethel, unequivocally.

Destined to die of boredom at the canasta table, Ethel was rejuvenated by Art. Both she and Bob wanted to collect paintings, but Ethel, of a more traditional bent, envisioned herself with perhaps a Rembrandt etching or a Cezanne watercolor. Bob liked modern and was especially intrigued by the outrageous works of a group of young men who later became known as Pop artists. One day, a huge van pulled up at the Scull home in Great Neck. The van door opened and the workmen unloaded an enormous painting. They staggered to the door with it as Ethel just stared. Smack in the center of a wild conglomeration of giant painted objects was a huge Spam sandwich. Into the house and onto the Sculls' walls went the work of art. "I bought the painting and I don't want to hear a word out of you," Bob told Ethel. "Live with it."

Soon Ethel and Bob were princess and prince of the Pop Art scene, buying works from wildly talented unknowns, holding court in the suburbs, ferrying out scruffy, paint-splattered artists on the Long Island Rail Road for a brunch in the country.

Culture commuting became Ethel's weekday salvation. Escape from the stifling suburbs by car or by train, run into the city, learn, study, absorb art: the Metropolitan, the Museum of Modern Art, Betty Parsons' gallery, a quick visit with dealer and friend Sam Kootz. And then, the Jewish momma's witching hour draws near. Ethel ran back to the suburbs to be home at three o'clock when the boys returned from school. Be there, or be guilty. Offer milk, cookies, a sympathetic ear, help with homework. Months passed and the schlep back and forth between two worlds proved too much for Ethel. She was ready for the big rebellion; she decided to move her contented suburban domicile back into the dirty city.

"I want to move back into New York," Ethel told Bob. She was greeted with silence. Finally Bob said, "I don't want to move. If you decide to do it, I'm not lifting a finger." Three little Scull princes sided with their daddy. Ethel's mother had a little fit: "You're supposed to be contented and fulfilled out there." But Ethel was fed up with life in the cultural wilderness, and in a reverse pioneer-woman role, she engineered a move back into civilization. In a one-woman display of hardy immigrant ancestry, she sold the house, furnishings and all, enrolled three boys in select private schools, transferred them to a new synagogue, and found an apartment. Virtually overnight, the old suburban skin was shed for new city chic. Perhaps not so chic, in Ethel's eyes. To this day, she refers to her Fifth Avenue digs as "my tenement." But she prefers what she believes are the "hardships" of city life (a less than magnificent apartment building, no grass and trees for the kids) to the luxury and ease of the custom-built, huge Great Neck house she left behind. Good-bye, L.I.

Ethel's Jewish Princess side served her well during the abrupt move back to the rigors of city life. She was able to decorate her new home single-handedly. Although the printed signs in many of the best furniture showrooms in Manhattan read "To the Trade Only," Ethel was undeterred. Armed with her decorator's card acquired in student days at the Parsons School of Design, she barged into store after store and ordered brand-new furnishings for her brand-new tenement. "But, madam," said a salesman, "we cannot have these beds delivered in two weeks. The order will take at least two months." Ethel drew up her slender figure, fixed her best Jewish momma look of concern and outrage on her face, and demanded, "Would you have my three little baby boys sleeping on the floor?" No salesman would. Two weeks later, the Sculls arrived, suitcases in hand, at their empty, half-painted barn of an apartment to find that only the beds had arrived. Ethel, excited, danced through her new home. "But four men followed me through the place, crying," Ethel recalls. "The boys said, 'Why did you bring us to this terrible place, Mommy?' And I told them that in six months, they'd thank me." After arriving at the apartment, Ethel marched right over to the phone, called Hertz, and rented everything else the family needed. Four morose men and one exhilarated Ethel bedded down that night in their new home.

The princess moved into her dream house, the start of a new era in her life, full of exciting people, the right parties, brilliant conversation and dominated by Art. The location of the dream palace? Superb. Right across the street from the Metropolitan Museum, no less, a stone's throw from the masterpieces of civilization. Ethel was in her element and she has thrived.

Ethel's Fiorentina-footed peer group of Manhattan Jewish Princesses live a programmed life of daily routines, shopping, lunching, exercising, entertaining. To Ethel, the customary route was anathema. She preferred the pursuit of Art and Artists. In the early sixties, a museum curator friend told the Sculls of a new find. "There's a nice boy I want you to meet, go visit him. His name is Andy Warhol. No one much likes his work." Better than a shopping trip, this was a voyage of discovery! Off went Ethel and Bob, down to a crowded Lexington Avenue studio. The atmosphere there was wonderful, Ethel recalls, cluttered and crowded, filled with outlandish paintings and presided over by this sweet, shy young man. They looked around, entranced. Soup cans, painted, hung on the wall. The Sculls fell in love with Andy's work. The three chatted excitedly for several hours and then Ethel and Bob announced they wanted to buy. Ethel recalls that Andy stood up and screamed that their interest was fantastic, but that he needed $1,400 and they could take anything they wanted. Oh no, Ethel and Bob protested, that wasn't what they had in mind, maybe just a few things. But Andy insisted and Ethel and Bob wandered through the studio. How like the couples strolling the aisles of Fraser-Morris on a crowded Saturday, stopping at the anchovies and then moving on to the caviar, making careful selections of coffee beans to be ground to order for their espresso maker. What a shopping trip! The experience of a lifetime. Ethel spotted a peeling soup can. "This is lovely," she said, and took it. Bob discovered one of a seven-cent stamp, and then another of dollar bills.

Their arms were soon full. Delighted with their selections, they took what they could carry and left the larger canvases to be picked up later. Ethel goes Beyond-Princess. Bob offered to buy her diamond jewelry. Ridiculous, Ethel told him and turned him down cold. "I'd rather have a painting. Buy me a De Kooning woman."

After years of sponsoring artists such as Robert Rauschenberg, Jasper Johns, Warhol, James Rosenquist, Ethel feels free to ask an artist to create a work for her home. The artists are her friends, whom she still calls "the boys." In Great Neck, there was a twelve-foot space on the Sculls' living room wall. What to do! Ethel and Bob asked Franz Kline to paint a canvas. Ethel has had her portrait done by Andy Warhol. "I didn't commission it, Bob did," Ethel is quick to note. "I'm not that vain." Apprehensive about the Warhol treatment at first (Ethel admits she was afraid she'd come out looking like a soup can), her nerves were calmed by Warhol's approach. He did not seat her on a stool in his studio and tell her not to move for three hours. Instead, he led her by the hand to a photo booth, the little chintzy picture-snapping ones found in dime stores that make three tiny snapshots for a quarter while you wait. The machine captured a series of Ethel posing, pouting, peering over and around a pair of large sunglasses. Then a batch of sultry looks and smiles sans glasses. The end product? "Ethel Scull Thirty-Six Times," a huge work composed of these selected little gems, blown up and tinted in lurid, carnival colors. A Warhol classic.

Dinnertime at the Sculls. "The boys" are frequent

guests. On a given night, Andy, Jasper or Bill might be munching roast beef and string beans along with the five Sculls. And Jonathan, Stephen or Adam Scull would hear, "Eat your dinner before it gets cold," interspersed with discussions of curators, galleries, MOMA and the latest art world gossip. Supper was a star-studded, select version of the ideal family meal, featuring what every Jewish parent wants his child to imbibe along with his whole milk: a little culture, a little knowledge. Ethel and Bob were the perfect patrons, relaxed around their friends, haimish. Why, Ethel even decorated Bill De Kooning's studio for him, "because he's a friend. I only decorate for other people out of friendship."

Over the years, the Sculls built up a superb art collection and a name for themselves as well-known collectors. Ethel, however, has remained steadfastly Ethel. She bristles at criticism that the Sculls are publicity-seekers and loyally defends their role in the art world. "Thank God there are people like us around today," she says, "who buy art out of love, who live with it. We helped the artists when they needed it." Sure she'd like to have more money, who wouldn't? But not for a Mercedes or a mink or a pied à terre in Paris. "We don't have all that much money. Look at Henry Ford. I'm not Ford, not that rich, but it would have been nice. Think of all the art we could have bought!"

Ethel, whose mother and husband told her to be contented and fulfilled as the lady of a Great Neck manse, is contented and fulfilled at last as patroness, art collector, artist's friend, presiding over her very own Fifth Avenue salon. She brushes aside the accoutrements of her very social New York life as unimportant; what matters to Ethel is what she and her husband have contributed to Art. And Ethel, golden-haired, beloved princess, points out rather morbidly, yet with a certain satisfaction, that immortality will be hers. The multiple portrait of Ethel by Andy Warhol will come to rest, after she dies, just across the street from her eleven-room abode, in the Metropolitan Museum of Art.

Ethel Scull is a Jewish Princess. But she is not your run of the mill, standard operating procedure princess. No, Ethel is ballsy, she has oomph, personality.

But Ethel is not the sole exception. Quite a few women possess proper Jewish Princess credentials but abhor the traditional role. If Ethel Scull is a different variety of Jewish Princess, then so is Abbie Zabar, for the same reasons. They share the failure to fit the stereotype. It's tough not to be what you're supposed to be.

Does the name Zabar ring a Pavlovian appetite bell? In the New York City area it does. Abbie married the scion of the great Zabar food clan, purveyors of a gargantuan array of tempting Jewish and not so Jewish gourmet nosh. They hit the edible retailing jackpot with a huge West Side store selling a mélange of traditional treats, lox, bagels, pickled herring and the like, cheek by jowl (or turkey wing by tongue) with imported goodies, Beluga caviar, crackers, jellies and fruits, bread, cake, candy and cheese. Zabar's, an eater's paradise, combines the best of the Old World pickle barrel and hanging salami school with the new era of French bread flown in by 747.

Abbie and husband Eli, in the best younger generation fashion for semi-rebellion, have set up their own much smaller food shop on the opposite side of Central Park, on Madison Avenue. E.A.T. (Eli and Abbie Together) as the store is cunningly known, isn't a copy of Daddy's place across town. The best bits from the bigger store, bagels, lox, cheese, gourmet specialties, are selectively mingled with home-cooked hors d'oeuvres and entrées and a line of continental kitchen hardware, wine racks, cookware, wooden spoons, mallets, all displayed in Old World fashion, in baskets and barrels, or on open wooden shelves. The epicurean inspiration is Eli's, the store design is Abbie's.

But Abbie is no shtetl-style wife, slaving along in her husband's business, pushing the pumpernickel or extolling the Edam. She works in the store for a few hours a day, the time she is not devoting to her "real" career, Art. A hardworking but undiscovered artist, Abbie looks less like a Soho woman than she does a small-town girl who hangs around the comic book racks at the local drugstore. She looks sixteen (she's actually twenty-nine), small and thin, dressed in jeans and T-shirt. With a white coat thrown over her clothes to work behind the counter, she seems to be playing Store. First impression? Shy, cautiously friendly, unprepossessing. But Abbie is full of surprises.

A man comes into the store, impatient in that way New Yorkers get when they want something done in a hurry. He barely notices the bright black and white tiled floor, the attractive display of cakes and breads in imported baskets, or the fat country stove in the rear issuing forth a mixture of heavenly cooking smells. He strides to the thick wooden table in front of a dairy cabinet and demands service. Abbie comes over. She smiles, she likes dealing with customers. What does that cheese taste like, he wants to know, and points to the Brie. Abbie always varies her answer with her mood. She has no standard New York brush-off salesperson reply. Nor is she cloyingly over-helpful. She searches for the right words, rolling her eyes toward the ceiling and waiting for the cheese muse to descend. Artistic, even in her counter service, she tries to find a creative way to talk about this squishy soft, tangy, ripe French cheese. But the impatient man can't wait. He bawls, "Anyone here who can help me who knows something about cheese?" He stalks away. Abbie shrugs her shoulders. She doesn't feel she has to like everyone or have everyone like her.

Abbie Wagman Zabar resists being classified as a Jewish Princess, a Jewish bride, a Jewish wife. But despite the resistance, she's loaded with a princess' Jewish chutzpah. Everything she does is backed by her own thorough confidence in herself. Everyone should be so sure. The confidence comes as a bit of a shock because Abbie looks so young and frail. But it's there.

Abbie actually stood up to her machetayneste. That's a pre-wedding struggle from which few Jewish Princesses emerge unscathed. But Abbie won her own way and she beat the Zabars on their own turf, no less, with food. Abbie insisted that a goyishly sparse amount of food be served at her wedding reception. It's hard to believe, but nice Jewish girl Abbie Wagman was given the run of Zabar's one day

41

five years ago to choose food for her wedding party and she rejected almost everything! The traditional Jewish wedding, with every possible permutation of food, could have been hers. But Abbie walked into Zabar's and looked at all that potato salad, coleslaw, Danish shrimp salad, lobster salad, chopped liver, cheese, bread, sliced meat, smoked salmon, lox, herring, cream cheese, bagels, the Jewish horn of plenty, and she said "No." What she wanted for her wedding party, to be held outdoors beneath a great striped tent, was Beluga caviar, champagne and sturgeon. Period. The Zabars could not believe it. Their very name is tantamount to food. They have catered thousands upon thousands of bar mitzvahs, engagement parties, weddings, and now Abbie Wagman was telling them no? It was as if Harry Winston's daughter-in-law had said no thanks to any diamond in the store. The postscript to this tale of food occurred on Eli and Abbie's wedding day, when Mrs. Zabar was discovered in the kitchen. Fearful that the guests would not have enough to eat, in wedding dress and all, she was cooking up a batch of chickens.

Abbie is not defined by the particulars of Jewish Princesshood; as the wedding story indicates she rejects many a princess' wildest dream. But Abbie is a princess still by dint of her upbringing. Without a second's hesitation, Abbie attributes her confidence, self-awareness and drive to the way she was raised, to her adoring mother. In the modest, middle class Wagman home, Abbie was star of the show. Mother thought she was very special, that whatever she did was "the best." In that hothouse atmosphere,

Abbie's talents were nurtured and encouraged. Her interest in art, for example, was aided by her mother's attention; Abbie would come home from school and find museum brochures and art school catalogues casually lying around the living room. And this mother, who thought Abbie was "really, really good" no matter what she did, provided the kind of ego boosting only a Jewish mother can give. "Remember, whatever you do, do it the best you possibly can," Mother said. "You're not supposed to settle for less." Abbie never forgot.

Secure in the knowledge that anything she applies her talents to will be a success, Abbie behaves with savoir faire, with grace under pressure. Her efforts bear fruit. Her success? The un-Jewish wedding menu was. The personalized store design is. And her barely budding art career will be. Not content to sit back and reap the rewards of an obviously marvelous catch, Abbie declined the role of Bagel Princess of the Zabar clan. She threw herself into the fray and set out to make E.A.T. "the best food store there has ever, ever been." Standing in the midst of the Madison Avenue location, without a blueprint in sight, she directed burly workmen to her specifications. "The floor is going to be tiled, shelves go here and there," she pointed out. Amazingly, the tough construction workers listened to the voice of conviction issuing from this small blue-jeaned girl. She pursues all of her plans to completion, finishing every project herself, even if it means her husband Eli has to cool his heels for her. For six months after their shop' opened, the store did business with a totally blank front window, with no store sign in sight. Against all laws of

43

retailing, Abbie put off doing the sign until she knew exactly what she wanted. Today, a year after the store opened, customers still march out with plain brown paper shopping bags. Anonymous parcels will have to suffice: Abbie's waiting for inspiration again, to do the paper bag design her way.

Abbie's strong inner drives surface intensely in her pursuit of her art career. Day after day, Abbie trudges to galleries, up and down the east side of Manhattan to dealer after dealer. Very nice, the gallery owners say, but no deals. Many compliments, no commitments, at best, discouraging, at worst, totally frustrating. Unbowed, Abbie plugs doggedly on with her paper on paper creations (called collage, a term which Abbie finds "tacky"), which consist of flat, almost abstract color areas fashioned into landscapes. Abbie believes her creations are worth a major show in a really good gallery and will not stop for less. An impossible dream? Not to hear Abbie tell it. "It's not what's wrong with me," she blankly states, "it's them. I'm confident if I like my work it's right. One day I know my things are going to be where I want them to be."

Even Mrs. Zabar, who cooked all those stopgap chickens, recognizes that Abbie is no standard Jewish Princess. She now proudly introduces her daughter-in-law as Abbie, the artist, and tries not to mention the word "grandchildren." Quite an achievement for a Jewish mother-in-law.

What Ethel Scull and Abbie Zabar share in common with other Jewish Princesses is a special kind of drive absent from the old stereotype. Jewish Princess Pizzazz,

44

something that cannot be purchased at Gucci, stamped with entwined initials. You've either got it or you don't. And that, in essence, is a guide to Jewish Princess-watching. She may come in various guises, walking the Lhasa apso, lugging the Bloomingdale's bag, schlumping along in jeans, bicycling by in a sweatsuit, but you can recognize her because she knows she's a Jewish Princess. And sooner or later, she'll let you know it, too.

3

DOWRY, DOWRY, WHO'S GOT THE DOWRY?

A Jewish Princess is born with a gold credit card in her mouth.

—Anonymous

The Jewish American Princess is the proud recipient of a dowry. Not the old ancestral funds of centuries past, money salted away often at great sacrifice by the parents to give to the nice boy who married her. No, she gets the American dowry, which goes straight on to the princess instead. A mile of wire is installed in her mouth, a small fortune is carved out of her nose, a tidy investment is made in clothes, hair and make up and then the princess is ready to go out and, please God, she should then only catch a husband.

Jewish American parents, whether or not they are well-to-do, feel compelled to spend money directly on the enhancement of their daughters. And the embellishing, primping and polishing of a princess is accompanied by constant reminders of The Ultimate Goal: "Get married, darling." This is a lesson she'll never forget. From the

47

moment of her birth there is a chuppah, a marriage canopy, swaying over her head. Her first present—the little white Bible, with her name embossed on the cover in gold. An innocuous enough gift, it seems. But wait, when the Jewish Princess is a curious five-year-old who spends her spare time plowing through her mother's bureau drawers, she finds the tissue-wrapped little book hidden amid the lingerie, and the indoctrination begins. "What's this?" asks the princess, holding up her new discovery. Her mother, cradling the telephone receiver as she interrupts her phone call, says, "Look at the mess you've made! Put my girdles back where you found them. That is your Bible, you'll carry it when you get married someday, God willing."

At the age of eight or nine, the little princess hears ominous reminders of her future goal dropped as subtly as leaden matzo balls. "Don't put your fingers in your ears," Mother says. "Who would want to marry someone who puts their fingers in their ears?" And as if dire warnings weren't enough, at age eleven the Jewish Princess begins her trial run-through, going the route of being "shown off" for company. Groomed, washed, pressed and dressed up, she is pulled into the living room where Mother's best friend Shirley sits with her itchy son Bernard. "Play the piano for him, darling," croons Mother. And she plays.

Even by the tender age of eleven or twelve, a Jewish Princess possesses a large number of items that fall into the category of new dowry. A glimpse of what the modern expenditure of funds represents is available at the

48

Friedman house, in the second floor bedroom of twelve-year-old Melissa. Missy is out, playing with friends down the street. Mother Myra and the maid have just tiptoed reverentially out of the cleaned and polished shrine to the little princess. Everything is quiet, a hush has descended, the air smells of lemon oil furniture polish and fresh linen. As the door closes behind Mrs. Friedman, Clovis (the maid), and the trundling vacuum cleaner, a breeze from the window ruffles the canopy over the bed. Permission has been granted to view Melissa's wardrobe, pressed and cleaned and hung and folded in her own little room. Obviously Mother and her "help" have straightened things up for the visit, but imagining a little twelve-year-old's untidiness does not change the picture very much. There is still enough here to boggle the senses.

Crossing the fluffy pink carpet over to the dresser, you pass by the bed, with its matching bedspread, dust ruffle and canopy in lacy pink and white pattern. The curtains and upholstered chair are done in the same fabric. Dresser, desk, night table and armoire are all in white antique wood with gold trim and gold fixtures. Even the plushy stuffed animals in one corner of the room are in various shades of matching pink and purple colors. But to the business at hand, Melissa's "dowry." Inside the drawers of the dresser are, first, piles of cotton underwear, in girlish colors of the rainbow, pressed (!). There is a pile of matching undershirts with tiny ribbons at the neck and another small drawer filled with socks, white, colored, ankle-length, knee high, and a pile of tights.

The dresser contains nightgowns and pajamas, all

flannel for winter in cunning patterns (dancing animals, sheep leaping fences, little tots yawning), an entire drawer of T-shirts ranging from chic (a rhinestone Minnie Mouse) to corny souvenirs (Hi! From Fort Lauderdale), and two drawers of sweaters, all astonishingly bagged in see-through plastic. They range from heavy knitted Alpine ski sweaters to soft cardigans with mother-of-pearl buttons (Grandma's idea of a little girl's gift).

But the closet is the show-stopper. The folding louvre doors pull back to reveal what must be the formal garden of closets, the Versailles of clothing symmetry. Every item is hung in descending size level, from tiny short skating skirt to long, floor-length tucked gingham bathrobe. In between are skirts, pants, blouses (colors separated from prints), ruffly party dresses and a fluffy white terry after-shower robe with a hood. There is not an enormous amount in the closet, but altogether it is a fair replica of an adult's collection of clothes if slightly miniaturized. Lined up on the floor of the closet are hiking boots, Hush Puppies, sneakers, black shiny rain boots, furry slippers (in pink, to match carpet), and small white wood Swedish clogs. On an overhead shelf, in plastic boxes, are patent leather Mary Janes, red leather loafers, brown suede tie shoes, ballet slippers, and riding boots.

A disclaimer must be issued here: This is not the child of a "rich" family. They are middle class, barely hedging into the upper brackets of their economic group, but they are by no means really wealthy. And what Melissa's closet reveals is not lavishly expensive clothes but rather a preoccupation with wardrobe, an enshrinement of wearing apparel. There is a single-mindedness of purpose about Melissa's grooming. And these attitudes did not come out of nowhere. They are a product of, if nothing else, the great concern Jewish families have with how other people see their daughters. As Mother always reminded her little girls, "You never know who you're going to meet."

In the first years of Jewish life in America, God forbid a little girl went out looking sloppy. The neighbors would talk. "Look at Mrs. Bloomenfeld's daughter, did you ever see anything like that? Doesn't anyone in that family take the time to put her in clean stockings? God knows where she's been in that dress. Like a ragpicker's child!" and they would cluck their tongues and shake their heads from side to side. Pressed and properly attired children brought grudging respect from equally upwardly mobile neighbors. Everyone made certain that his children had the best of everything, or appeared as though they did. In the 1920's, on a subway ride home from a shopping trip to S. Klein's, Union Square headquarters for garment bargains, one mother pulled a Saks Fifth Avenue bag out of her bundles and switched the coat she bought for her daughter from its Klein's wrapping to a more suitable, high-class Name bag. Then the two walked home from the subway, Momma holding the bag before her like a victory banner. E Pluribus Saks Fifth Avenue.

Today the nosy neighbors on the front stoop are gone, but the legacy lingers on. "Ma, I'm going out to buy some Tampax," hollers Marcia. "Aren't you going to put on any lipstick?" queries her mother. "I forgot it," says Marcia.

"Look inside the pocket of your raincoat," Mother trills. Marcia's hand comes out with a fuzzy wad of Kleenex, a crumpled pack of cigarettes, and a tube of Yum-Yum Tangerine. "Listen, I paid $4,000 to have her teeth fixed and she goes out with her face looking so white? I'll show you something else, look," and from the pocket of Marcia's pea coat, her mother produces another slender gold cylinder, this time Cinnamon Toast. Marvelous how these mothers operate. Marcia never had a chance.

The right appearance overrides almost anything else in its overwhelming importance for the Jewish mama. One Jewish mother watched her daughter win more than $5,000 on the NBC-TV game show *Jeopardy* several years ago and after the four TV appearances were over, called her daughter on the phone. "Hello, darling," the mother said. "Did you watch?" asked the exuberant young woman. "I saw it," her mother said. "You should have worn a different bra."

The first major investment of the princess' new dowry is in clothes. Perhaps because of her garment industry, sweatshop heritage, the Jewish Princess is kept far from a needle and thread. She does not learn to sew her clothes, rather she learns to shop, a talent worlds away from the middle American zigzags of a Singer sewing machine. To a Jewish mother, shopping is not an activity, it is a learned skill with a set of instructions, rules and secret codes that are passed down from generation to generation. The course of study is not completed until a daughter is permitted to use her mother's department store charge plates on her own. Then, and only then, does a Jewish

Princess really enter the Big Leagues, shopping with the real heavyweights.

To shop or not to shop is a major childhood battling point. Carol Abelson, twelve years old, knows that a shopping excursion means an entire afternoon of picking over a variety of outfits and accessories, trailing around behind her mother and suffering general exhaustion at day's end. Her mother, Rhoda, is firm. "We're going." Climbing into the family's country squire station wagon, they set off from Tenafly, New Jersey, to a nearby shopping mall in Paramus to do the stores. Though Mother has on occasion sent clothes home for Carol to try on and accept or reject, Carol's presence is becoming essential on these expeditions. As Carol haltingly moves from pubescence to adolescence, her mother becomes increasingly aware that some day her daughter will be on her own and forced to shop solo. In many Jewish families, such separation never occurs; mothers and daughters remain joined by umbilical price tags until one or the other passes away. But Rhoda Abelson, trim in a sharkskin pants suit, auburn hair pulled into a small ponytail at the nape of her neck, is modern and ponders Carol's Future Independence. Carol, dressed in T-shirt and jeans with unwashed hair, a spill of frizzes in a Jewish Afro, sulks on the other side of the car.

Entering the cool bustle of a suburban department store, with its chiming sales manager bells and rattling shopping bags, mother and daughter proceed to the Junior Miss departments. A new winter coat is today's featured presentation and Rhoda plunges in. With Carol at her side, class is in session. "Look at this one, classic A-line, it will give you a lot of use. But I don't like the way the material feels. See? Not warm enough." Screech goes that hanger, down the metal bar. "Not fully lined. No good." Screech! "Now this would be adorable, see it's in a neutral color, a gray goes with your patent leather shoes and those red boots. Oh, it's darling. But the houndstooth plaid meets funny under the arms. Badly made. And no extra buttons." Screech! Thirty minutes pass as styles and manufacturers are reviewed. Carol has not tried on more than two coats or said more than five words, but the inspection process teaches her the ropes. A coat is a major purchase and, as with other moderately big investments, pants suits, or skirts and jackets, Carol is taught to "buy good, so they'll last." Later on, in advanced training, Mother plans to take Carol into "the city" to uncover the ins and outs of buying wholesale at various manufacturers' outlets. After exploring the list of "connections," the final stop will be several discount clothes operations. There, Carol will learn to interpret the hieroglyphics used when a Geoffrey Beene or Halston is sold stripped of its inside label but with a hint of its origins buried somewhere on its attached sales ticket.

Advanced Clothes Consciousness II is a very successful Jewish training course. In Briarcliff Manor, a very well-to-do, predominantly gentile Westchester enclave, the senior class of Briarcliff High traditionally voted one girl in the class "Best Dressed." Year after year the winner was usually Jewish. Despite all of the gentile money floating around town, the non-Jewish girls rarely had a chance.

Their parents didn't give them the gorgeous wardrobes. So one of the mere handful of Jewish girls in the senior class most often walked away with the title. The girls were well dressed because their mothers really cared. One mid-sixties Miss Best Dressed from Briarcliff was Paula Cantor. A high school photograph shows Paula with her hair in a "flip" (turned up in a curl just below ear level), wearing a perfectly coordinated outfit of madras skirt, Oxford blue shirt and matching Pappagallos. Looking at Paula today, there is little evidence to prove she represented anyone's notion of best dressed. Where did it all go? No Pucci pajamas here, Paula is wearing cut-up jeans and her husband's frayed shirt as she sits in her dining "L" and feeds her ten-month-old daughter a dribbling dose of oatmeal. Yeah, says Paula, being well dressed was her mother's idea. Momma taught her how to buy *good* in all of the best stores. But after talking with Paula for a little while, Mother Cantor's lessons creep out. "I can't even go out to buy a work shirt today without finding the best work shirt possible," Paula moans. And where, do tell, does an ex-Best-Dressed Princess buy a work shirt? "My husband knows that if I shop anywhere, it's going to be Bendel's, Bergdorf's or Bonwit's." The lady has clearly learned her lessons.

Unfortunately, here and there are Jewish Princesses who overlearn their shopping skills. They are a bit too eager, like the Washington, D.C., girl who serves as a case in point. We will call her Linda Lovelabel, for obvious reasons. Perhaps because of her Washington roots, she waxes political about her feelings: "It's important to me to have the right things, the in things. I'll never buy discount clothes in a place where they remove the good labels. What's the point of buying then? That's as bad as the Watergate tapes, with the expletive deleted parts. All the good stuff has been cut out!" Linda was the girl who received a gag present in junior high school of a box filled with labels. "A scream. And in the bottom, inner soles from my favorite brand of shoes." Undeterred by that birthday gift, Linda's fame in high school grew, based on her purple suede Gucci rain shoes. "That's right, Gucci. I kept them in my locker for bad weather. They were such an *unusual* color they didn't really go with anything I had."

Linda's many talents include proficiency at coat and jacket folding, an acrobatic twist which enables the owner of a chic outer garment to display its origins with ease. Flip the coat inside out, turn it neatly in half and place over the back of a chair. The rest of the room is now enlightened as to its store origins. Designer scarves and Vuitton tote bags have eased Linda's folding chores momentarily. Happy with her status purchases, she wears her bags, belts, buckles and bangles daily, secure in the knowledge that they spell chic at a glance.

In college, Linda sported the "$90 T-shirt, $10 jeans look," embellishing her nothing-hip outfits with a single article of good fashion faith. Tattered jeans, polo shirts, and Army surplus raincoat were worn with an alternating symbol of class, a pair of intricately laced Spanish leather boots, a handmade imported tote bag for books, or her tiny gold earrings and slender gold chain. Linda has the pattern down, all right. When a group of students from her Vassar art history class spent a summer in Florence, Linda did not waste a moment. Said a member of the study group, "We went to the Uffizi, she went to Gucci."

But then, why shouldn't Linda operate with such precision? She was programmed to be an ambitious groomer. At sixteen, she had a little plastic surgery on her nose, which her mother euphemistically called a correction for a "deviated septum," but we who know best say "nose job." The operation did not satisfy Linda and so she had a second. Her parents believed that the net worth of Linda's appearance overrode any other financial considerations and so, at eighty dollars a throw, Linda flew to Washington twice monthly from school at Poughkeepsie, New York, to have her hair properly streaked, conditioned and cut by her very own hairdresser, Jean Claude. No one else would do, least of all the heathen hairdressers in upstate New York. And Momma and Poppa paid for these things, just as they now do for a decorator and an electrician to transform the extra walk-in closet in Linda's bedroom at home into a fully-lit, mirrored makeup room.

Parents become accustomed to doing such things for their daughters as though they were taking out some form of matrimonial insurance. "If she's not so gorgeous, well, we'll make her gorgeous, knock on wood, we've got the means to do it." And in addition, Jewish parents are always eager to take advantage of modern advancements in technology that they find beneficial. Like the nose job. Modern medical science marches on and the Jewish mother is right behind. Parents are not afraid to turn to a doctor for major surgical help. They run to physicians at the drop of a Kleenex anyway, so why not let Dr. Silver make their little bubeleh more gorgeous? Nose jobs were common operations for loads of princesses still in high school. "Okay, guess what we're going to do over Christmas. We're not going to Miami this year. No, not Puerto Rico either. We're going to get your nose done!" Critics charge those battered, black-eyed and bandaged survivors of the profile battle with attempting to disguise a Semitic appearance. But does anyone mean to say that Susan Schwartz is going to be less Jewish because she had her nose fixed? What she is going to be is prettier. So Susan takes off Christmas vacation and has the operation, returning to school looking remarkably better. Susan's boyfriend is enthusiastic. "It made her gorgeous. See, a pretty girl becomes beautiful and a so-so girl becomes pretty. Mostly, it makes her more of a princess because now she really knows she's something."

But plenty of girls are princesses with unfixed noses. And Susan Schwartz already knows she's really "something" without any help from a plastic surgeon. Sit down opposite her in a coffee shop and watch as she takes twenty minutes to decide she really fancies a hamburger today, thank you. And then the waitress finally brings her order and she sends back the Coke because the glass is smudged and takes her hamburger plate in front of her, sweeps aside the french fries, and, wrinkling her nose, carefully peels off a slice of tomato. Why do you do that? you ask as she places the roll back on the burger and prepares to eat. "Because," says Susan as she sweeps her long hair over her shoulders and out of the way of her "new" nose, "I don't like winter tomatoes."

Dowry, Dowry, Who's Got the Dowry?

Jewish Princesses who possess that kind of interior cool are not having their profiles altered for psychological value; they're not getting securer, they're looking better. In Brooklyn, they call it "polish," something many young women are expected to acquire when they are sent to Europe for the summer after their senior year of high school. "Aren't you sending Jane to Switzerland for polish?" one mother asks another at their local A&P. Not taken by that particular notion, Jane's mother says, "No," and with a sweep of her arm indicating the shelves of Pledge, Jubilee and Endust, says, "It's right here for her to get it."

If it isn't Switzerland for the summer, a mother will have some plan in mind to make her daughter Ready, some technique designed to implant the standard Boy Scout "Be Prepared" logic into her daughter's recently coiffed head. It gets so that princesses never go anywhere without a variety of interior neon signs lighting up and flashing on and off, somewhere between their ears: *Comb hair, lipstick on, jeans, no! Pants suit, yes!* Whether these efforts pay off is a more complicated question, to be explored in the context of dating, but some evidence exists to indicate that negative feedback can occur. Too much concern with the elements of the new dowry defeats its purpose entirely. To wit, one of the oldest Jewish Princess jokes floating around goes like this. The scene is in bed. He: "Can I do anything?" She: "Sure, as long as you don't touch my hair. I just had it done."

Further proof of a kind of Jewish Princess grooming backlash was overheard in a Manhattan living room. Gathered around a fireplace in one bachelor's studio apartment were six terrific catches, swinging singles planning a coed summer house on Fire Island. "We gotta advertise," says the accountant. "Put an ad in the *Village Voice*," the lawyer suggests. "What'll we say?" asks the stockbroker. "I know," says the public relations director. "Groovy women invited but no Jewish Princesses who'll monopolize the bathroom." End on great titters of knowing self-satisfaction.

But the gentlemen soon learn that there is a great seriousness of purpose behind all of the flashing lipsticks and combs. The Talmud counseled families to "sell even the holy scrolls to make sure a poor girl has a dowry." In America the investment has swelled to even greater proportions and no Jewish Princess is allowed to let all of that time, money and effort go to waste. So another little neon sign lights up inside her head, high above the others, shining bright and clear. It says *Date=Mate*. The six Fire Island swingers should only know what's in store. They will not be laughing for long.

4

THE MATING DANCE

From The New York *Times* paid social announcements column, 1973 (the names have been changed):

WEDDINGS: Mrs. Irving Horowitz and the late Irving Horowitz joyfully announce the marriage of their daughter Michelle to Ronald Levine, son of Mr. and Mrs. Bernard Levine.

The Jewish Princess' social debut is no fancy dress ball lined with tuxedoed escorts clasping dozens of arms swathed in long white gloves. Instead, there's a continuously nudgy momma who gives the princess time, attention, encouragement, culture, straight Hollywood starlet teeth and stunning drop-dead outfits and then pushes her daughter straight into the arms of the right match.

Jewish mating: the magic moment of the first date. Mother is right in there pitching. She takes her fifteen-year-old daughter to sit at the local pool club and hatches plans for the princess to meet "someone nice." "Did you know that the busboy over there is going to

Columbia University next year?" The daughter is ready to make a dive under the chaise lounge. "Here goes Mother again," the girl thinks, and she shrugs and feigns indifference. "Well, if you won't go over there, I will," and with that Momma walks over to the harried, sweaty tray schlepper. "See that girl over there?" she says sotto voce. "The one reading *War and Peace*. That's my daughter. Go talk to her. She's very smart. Gets A's in school."

Whatever parents do for their daughters to aid and abet the snaring of a husband falls into the category of "Mating Dance." But unlike the genteel cool of the goyish fancy deb ball or coming out party, the Mating Dance has an edge of heartburn—Jewish aggravation. A good part of the tsuris is attributable to the traditional belief that only if married is a Jewish girl truly happy. Indeed, the sum total of Jewish wisdom on the subject of marriage is that being single is sinful.

Jewish parents feel somehow responsible for matchmaking. Somebody has to take care of their little girl and since there are no professional matchmakers around anymore, Momma and Poppa have designated themselves official American shadchens. If the right matches are not made in heaven as shtetl folk believed, then parents will make them right here on earth, on the corner of Delancey and Essex if necessary.

Robbed of the matchmakers' little black book of suitable bachelors, Jewish parents devised their own mating list to enable their daughters to Pick Right. A Jewish Princess cannot marry just anyone. If she is to be exquisitely happy, and her parents will not settle for anything less, she must date and mate someone who meets two specific qualifications: Jewish and better. First, "He should be a nice Jewish boy." (Of course, in the language of Jewish parents, nice has a meaning all its own. In how many delicatessens do you hear people asking for "nice pastrami?" They don't mean just all right, they mean "The best," or else.) But of course Jewish. Parents will not hear of anything else and they drive the point home hard.

Making certain a boy is Jewish entails close supervision. Jewish girls rarely have any kind of contact with a young man without some version of this query popping up: "Oh, so you had a Coca-Cola together. That's nice. Is he Jewish?"

But nice and Jewish alone does not suffice. So up the Jewish ladder they climb to "better." He is better if he makes more money than her father, a healthy income to support the princess in royal style. The princess' parents make certain he knows the stakes. "A maid? Can you afford a maid? Or a second bathroom? You gonna be able to give her a second bathroom?" If he can afford it, that's "better." The perfect match, however, does not only earn money, he also possesses Jewish clout, i.e., education. The ideal better Jewish catch is a professional man.

Doctors are the first and foremost candidates for the hand of the Jewish Princess. They've got the perfect mix, years of concentrated learning, walls of laminated degrees, public respect and, of course, they make a lot of money. "Ever heard of a poor doctor?" asks Momma. John Jacob Astor steps aside for Dr. Marvin Schwartz, urologist. At a recent canasta game, one mother brought the playing and kibbitzing to a standstill with news of her daughter's social conquest. "She's dating such a nice boy," the mother said. "Who is he?" asked her eager card partners. Beaming, Mother said, "A premedical student." An "Ahhh" of bliss filled the room as the ladies kvelled. However, not every princess kvells as easily. One problem with MDs is that pickier princesses may reject them as unsuitable husbands, as did the wife of a chairman of the board: "I never liked doctors. I never wanted to marry someone who would have an operation the night I was having a dinner party."

Next in the professional lineup are dentists ("Almost a doctor," as one knowing mother said), followed in short order by lawyers, accountants (only if they're CPA's), stockbrokers (in a bull market), and men in Daddy's business, if classy and lucrative enough. Every American princess (from protected progeny of the twenties to the liberated ladies of today) has learned the list. There is something eternal about the choices, something final. But finding an available gastroenterologist for your daughter was not always easy and each generation concocted its own surefire formula for making their Estelle a Mrs.

The first Jewish parents to try their hand at New World matchmaking stuck close to home. Pre-World War I families sent out feelers in the neighborhood, contacting friends and relatives to scout out a nice boy from a good Jewish family who maybe even went to CCNY! Mating was a dull business for the princess and prince in those days. Satisfactory bachelors were permitted to enter the sanctity of the family home and keep company for endless months with the carefully watched Jewish Princess.

64

The Mating Dance

In the 1920's and 1930's, the real fun of the Mating Dance began. Activity moved out of the front parlor and into the swinging kosher social whirl. Parents began to regard Jewish Princesses as portable merchandise and took them Everywhere. To bar mitzvahs, to weddings, to temple dances, and to Aunt Bertie's living room. There, parents could keep a watchful eye on their daughter's social life and provide on-the-spot encouragement or discouragement when needed. Even better still, Jewish families in the thirties made a major social discovery: the Catskills resort. Grossinger's was the thriving, happy hunting ground for the Jewish Princess and her mother. No other place offered a selection of one hundred percent grade A certified Jewish men along with all ten-course meals. A Jewish Princess sitting down to lunch could select pickled herring and a podiatrist in the same breath. And there was plenty of time to become intimate over stuffed derma or kasha varnishkes, ample opportunity to wear a dozen new outfits and a chance to show off your fox-trot lessons. Marjorie Feldman, Manhattan Jewish Princess circa 1937, spent her unhappiest unmarried days being schlepped to huge Catskills monuments.

Arriving at Grossinger's late one Friday evening for the two-week stay, nineteen-year-old Marjorie, her two sisters, ages sixteen and twenty-one, and their mother, spent several hours unpacking. Out of the trunk came the bathing suits, the bathing robes, the beach slippers, tennis shorts, "play" suits, luncheon dresses, evening gowns, shoes, stockings, gloves, jewelry, hats, sunglasses, tennis racquets, bathing caps. And the iron. Mother pressed, daughters slept. Came the dawn, the first stirrings. "Out of bed," yelled Momma. "I didn't bring you here to sleep." Off went the girls, to a huge breakfast, and then Momma's specialty, a walk in the lobby. Up and down they walked, white pleated skirts flying as they covered every inch of the lobby. Mother watched each guest's arrival like a hawk, looking for old friends, remembered poolside acquaintances with male children. Spotting a familiar face coming in, she turned to her daughters and yelled, "Look who's coming in, girls. Girls? Get over here now, fast. It's Mrs. Margolies." The three came out from behind a screen of potted palms and slowly walked to their animated mother, busy greeting her friend. "Hello there, Mrs. Margolies. That's Martin? He's gotten so tall." Martin, carrying a set of golf clubs, looked at his feet. "Say hello, girls," Mother said, and walked behind them to urge them forward. "Behave, or I'll give you such a smack!" she said in an angry whisper.

Back to the room they went, a quick zip out of morning outfits and into poolside numbers, flowery robe over bathing suit, and down to the swimming pool, to sit. Not to swim. "I made the mistake of going in the water once," Marjorie said, "and my mother came over and saw me and screamed loud enough for everyone to hear, 'Look what you're doing to your hair!' " Back to their room next, change, tennis lessons, back to the room, press, change for lunch. Another walk through the lobby, lunch, and then golf lessons in the afternoon. In a state of exhaustion at dinner time, the girls made up, climbed into evening dresses and rushed downstairs to secure their table by the dance floor, front and center, where the girls would be able to see all available dancing partners. Soon the dining room filled with what looked like ten million girls, and five million mothers, anxiously waiting for someone to ask their daughters to dance, the girls wolfing down soup, salad, rolls, quickly before the waiters snatched them away. A young man came over to ask Marjorie to dance and she said no. "No? You said no?" Mother was aghast. "I didn't bring you here to sit and eat." If the girls failed to obey their mother, Momma would give them a knip on the arm, nice and hard. A knip, Jewish mother's convincing specialty, is a pinch on the upper part of the arm, a twisting of flesh to serve as a reminder or purpose. "I used to come home all black and blue from those weeks away," Marjorie says.

Now a married mother in her fifties, not terribly stylish or chic, with unlacquered graying hair, two daughters and an adoring husband, Marjorie says she never did meet anyone at Grossinger's. "But if you didn't meet, it was back home, to try and find someone in the neighborhood. Mother was so anxious for all of us to meet people that she had us constantly in motion." The neighborhood was Manhattan's Upper West Side, an area known in those days as the "Jewish half mile," Broadway and West End Avenue in the eighties and low nineties with its concentration of middle and upper middle-class Jewish families. Schrafft's on Broadway and Eighty-third Street was a popular watering hole. Marjorie and sisters dressed to the teeth to go for a stroll on Riverside Drive, with Momma right behind them, and then retire to Schrafft's for ice-cream sodas. (No sundaes, chocolate syrup stained lipsticked mouths and good clothes.) The eldest daughter Rita, girl most likely to be married first, often had arranged introductions waiting and she got to wear the best clothes. The nicest handbag, the good jewelry, the newest scarf were donated by sulky, unwilling siblings, who watched in amazement one Sunday as Rita snared Sammy, the garment manufacturer's son. Those were the days, Marjorie reminisces, when the three sisters, all extremely tall, nearsighted and de-eyeglassed for social occasions, were described as "gorgeous" by their loving, anxious mother. "My mother once met Jolie Gabor at an airport and said, 'You know, I have three beautiful daughters at home, just like you.'"

This carefully chaperoned version of the Mating Dance took place in several large cities during the 1930's and early 1940's. The urban mating scene was a Jewish parent's dream. They could keep an eye on their daughter and at the same time, see that she met lots of nice boys. But just when Mother and Father thought they could sleep more easily, the economic and social turn of events following World War II contributed to the great Move to the Suburbs. Jewish families were off and running out of New York, Philadelphia, Chicago, Boston and Cleveland, and into gentile riding and golfing turf in grassy outlands beyond the cities. Thus the gilded ghetto came into existence, Jewish suburbia: split levels, paneled dens, artful landscaping, two-car garages *and* brand-new synagogues, culture groups, restricted Jewish country clubs, hyperactive PTA's. The appearance of gilded ghettos signaled the start of a new mating era. Freedom. The old chaperoning of the city seemed out of place in the leafy privacy of suburbia. Few girls walked the unsidewalked streets with their mothers in tow; everyone rode everywhere in his own car. And girls needed less watching socially because almost everyone they met was Jewish. Nervous parents should have relaxed in this atmosphere: but they didn't.

Anxious as ever, Jewish parents still wanted a hand in the mating process. The ethnic purity of their new surroundings did not satisfy them. After all, how could their daughter know whether or not Arthur Goldfarb from down the block was really a schlemiel or a potential money-maker? In order to have some say over just exactly who took their precious princess out, suburban parents became extremely fond of blind dates—those they arranged themselves, naturally. Suburban phone wires buzzed with the sound of mommas giving out names, phone numbers and descriptions. "My Marcia? You'd never recognize her now. She's just gorgeous." Mother's friend would then call her friends and find a nice boy. Once a catch was located, *his* family took over. "A girl from Mamaroneck," his mother enthused. "Think of it, Harry. They must have a lot of money." The family began working hard to persuade the prince. "Take her out, she's the greatest thing since sliced bread," the parents would say. "Go out with her. It'll make me so happy, I'll buy you a present," this, from Momma. Daddy is more direct, "Take the girl out, what can it hurt? I'll give you two hundred dollars." To which one prince replied, "Are you kidding? For a princess two hundred dollars isn't enough."

In the 1950's, parents were still able to preselect suitable young men, as did Mr. Morgenstern, a case in point. Proprietor of an office supply business, Mr. Morgenstern used the store to supply his daughter with a stream of nice, eligible young men setting up their new offices. When one of these professionals entered the store, Mr. Morgenstern rushed up to help him. "Oh, just setting up business, I see, I see," Mr. Morgenstern said. Then, the questions. "You a lawyer? Oh, an accountant. Here are some nice adding machines. CPA? Oh, that's very good. Married? Why not, a nice Jewish boy like you?" Several weeks later, when the shipment of brand-new furniture arrived at the accountant's new office, inside the top left-hand drawer of the shiny wood desk lay Mr. Morgenstern's business card with a large red "Over" printed neatly on the front. On the other side of the card, inked in red, was "Rita Morgenstern, WH 6-9883."

You can lead a prince to a business card but you can't make him call. So Jewish mothers often resorted to more surefire methods to grab a good match. Mrs. Kapelowitz, Shaker Heights Momma extraordinaire, kept one ear pressed close to the kosher butcher grapevine for news of single MD's and LD's setting up practice in her city. Word got out about a young lawyer taken in by an excellent firm. Within two weeks of his arrival, Mrs. Kapelowitz had called and invited him to participate in a Bonds for Israel fund-raising drive. She hit pay dirt: the lawyer, Stephen Richter, was a kosher Zionist. After a look-over at a bond drive meeting, Mrs. K. invited Stephen to her house for dinner, ostensibly to discuss further fund-raising activities. "Boy was I relieved when I got asked there," said Stephen.

"I'd been in Cleveland three weeks and every night I got another invitation to go to someone's house and meet a sister, daughter, niece, cousin. But here I thought, I'm being invited for myself." The next night, walking into the Kapelowitz living room, Stephen met his raison d'être: Pamela Kapelowitz. Fuzzy-haired, gopher-faced Pam. After a lavish pot roast and kasha, challah and Jello fruit mold dinner, Pamela's father stood up, stretched and said to his daughter, "I'm tired, but get your things and I'll take you into the city." Pam was spending the night at her married sister's (status duly noted by Mrs. Kapelowitz) and Stephen, well-trained Jewish boy, rose to the occasion. "Manners, I always had. I offered to take her there." Mrs. Kapelowitz crooned, "Oh, isn't that nice," and, loading her daughter and Stephen up with shopping bags of clean laundry and food, quickly ushered the two to the door, kissed them good-bye and closed the door on their departing backs. Stephen said he heard a great sigh of relief from inside the house. Driving quickly, he arrived at Pamela's destination, lugged her and her shopping bags to the top floor of the building and left hurriedly.

Two weeks hence, late for a fund-raising dinner at a large hotel ballroom, Stephen rushed in and asked the gardenia-corsaged "hostess" where he was seated. Given a card for his table, he headed into the smoky, jammed room where the guests had already passed from gefilte fish to mushroom and barley soup. Table 8: three married couples, an empty chair, and Pamela Kapelowitz, daughter of who else but Mrs. Kapelowitz, chairman of the seating committee.

Arranging a blind date was only the tip of the parental iceberg in the fifties; when the princess had a date, anyone would think the parents were going along, too. Mother ran from room to room with a hot iron, pressing anything in sight that moved and wrinkled. Father changed his shirt twice, shaved for a second time that day, and laid in a supply of ginger ale in the icebox. The Jewish Princess, in the eye of the storm, was made perfect for the moment when Mr. Imperfect walked in and submitted to Inspection. Not content with merely supervising their daughter's dates, Jewish parents also had to give them the Kosher Housekeeping seal of approval. The Once-Over was designed to answer only one question, but it was a lulu: "Will he make our daughter happy, even if they're only going to the movies?"

In the 1950's, when freer life-styles and hipper dress were yet to be tolerated, the prince was considered perfect if he wore shined loafers, clean white socks, impeccable pressed button-down shirt, and lint-free cardigan sweater. He had to look "Ivy League," though he may have been far from Harvard or Yale. Ivy League was synonymous with good taste in the fifties; it meant that *his* mother cared, and spent time pressing him. Another quick check was made when Father entered the room (well-mannered princes leaping up to shake hands) and crossed to the front window to pull back the drapes and see if the boy was driving his father's Cadillac, a big car, always safer. Then, the questions: What temple do you belong to? Is your mother in Hadassah or Sisterhood? What did you do last summer? How much money did you make caddying?

Which golf club? Then there were the extremes. One Brooklyn father even looked up a young man's father's Dun and Bradstreet rating. Mercifully the hosiery business was doing well that winter and the rating was acceptable. All of these questions, however, bred rebellion in the soul of the prince, even though he smiled and answered every question politely. "The scene was always the same, not a bit subtle. The parents always said, 'Where do you live? Oh, fine. What does your father do? Oh, very nice.' Then they passed knowing looks. But I always wanted to say, 'My father? He was rubbed out in the St. Valentine's Day Massacre.'" Poor soul, standing there in his Bass Wejuns, he never got his chance to use the punch line. But it's just as well. Anxious Jewish parents might have misunderstood what he said and thought he was a Catholic.

For the Jewish Princess, tired of conducting her social life in the controlled atmosphere of the family laboratory, there was always college to look forward to, right? Wrong. Getting away from home to attend school out of town was hardly an escape from the dictates of the Mating Dance. The operative idea of college was to get the bachelor's degree and the bachelor, finish marching down one aisle and then a quick switch to another. Parents made the point clear. "College," said a former Cornell coed of the fifties, "was supposed to determine the man I'd marry. Mother told me to join a good Jewish sorority. If you did you'd meet guys from the right fraternities. If you wanted a husband with good background and money, the fraternities just preselected them for you."

If a fifties Jewish Princess encountered husband-hunting difficulties at college, she had a quick remedy at her disposal: transferring. A lemminglike mass movement occurred at many schools after Jewish girls suffered through "Sophomore Slump," the second-year low point in their social lives. Wave upon wave of princesses packed up and transferred, fleeing the rah-rah isolated campuses for sophisticated city schools deep in the heart of medical, law and dental student territory. A former Syracuse University student government leader presided over special hearings devoted to the problem of Stemming the Sophomore Tide. "We had emergency sessions because the turnover of Jewish girls got bigger every year. But no one could think of ways to keep them from leaving. There weren't enough of us to go out with all of them."

Life in the fifties is the stuff of nostalgia today but the reputation of the Jewish Princess as an avid mating dancer has not faded into fond memory. Through the swinging sixties and into the stoned seventies, the Jewish Princess marches to the same drummer her counterparts heard in the forties and fifties: her mother. On college campuses today, a good number of Jewish girls represent a kind of throwback to an earlier era. Yeshiva College students still say that Stern College women are "getting their M.R.S. degrees." At Boston University? "The Jewish Princess enrolls in pre-wed." On the University of Cincinnati campus, where the famed rabbinical training school the Hebrew Union College sits, Jewish girls attend classes anxious to make that most traditional match. "My classmates first thought I was there, like them, looking for a rabbi for a husband," Rabbi Sally Priesand says of her sixties college days. "They didn't realize I was there to *become* one."

Locked in the body of an up-to-date, well-educated 1970's model Jewish Princess are the old tribal yearnings. The impulses, ingrained since childhood, are impossible to discard. Wendy Schuman has tried. Production editor on a women's magazine, Wendy has gone to consciousness raising sessions and women's liberation raps and still finds her upbringing wins every time. "Whenever a friend of mine calls to announce she's engaged, I immediately think, what's her diamond ring like? How many carats? Is she having a big wedding? Sometimes I even ask. I know I'm not supposed to feel the way I do, but I can't help it even though I know it's silly."

No matter how hip a current-day princess looks, chances are she behaves as though Momma were right behind her, ready to give her a quick knip on the arm. But the seventies princess follows a path which is a bit different. Like Barnard student Andrea Bergman, a crusader on any issue affecting the Jewish people. Andrea admits that no cause is so important as to exclude a little mating from its ranks. Blue jeaned Andrea, with her book bag, bicycle and frizzy unset hair pushed under a peasant scarf, does not march for protest alone. "My girl friends and I do look for guys at certain functions." Which ones? "Oh, the Salute to Israel parades, Jewish Defense League rallies, Soviet Jewry picketings, political lectures at the Lincoln Square Synagogue. You don't really go to hear what some rabbi has to say about amnesty or abortions. You really look over the prospects." "Yeah," Andrea's current boyfriend adds, "she stopped going since she met me." Chance encounters at political meetings and rallies lead to a cup of coffee later or a trip downtown to a kosher Chinese restaurant. Andrea's parents would beam at a job well done: a night in temple followed by rabbinically approved Moo Goo Gai Pen.

Although picketing, birth control pills, coed beach houses and women's lib all grow in the Jewish Princess' garden, they remain dwarfed by the hardy perennial, husband-hunting. No radical political, social or sexual revolutions, in my opinion, have altered the basic pattern of the Mating Dance. Parents, the perpetuators of the whole business, claim everything is different. But don't listen to them. Ask their daughters. Even if Momma and Poppa insist that their daughter is an independent, carefree girl, they are closing their eyes to a few crucial facts, and to their subconscious wish for grandchildren. They raised their daughter to get married, please God, and although they can breezily brush aside the years of training, she usually cannot. The mating commandments come carved in stone: "Seek and ye shall find," "A half-carat ring is bupkes," "Make sure he washes his hands before dinner," "Always wear clean underwear."

Sit down and have a nice talk with Ellen Finklestein, a twenty-six-year-old Jewish Princess who phones her mother only twice a week, probably some kind of record. All the same, Ellen lives in a parentally-approved, white-walled, forty-story "luxury" building on the Upper East Side of Manhattan. Her apartment is unluxurious despite central air conditioning, a dishwasher and plush wall-to-wall carpeting. The closets are painfully small and filled to bursting with shoes, handbags, skirts, sweaters, slacks, fun furs, Ellen's winter wardrobe (spring and summer clothes lie in state in garment bags at her mother's). Ms. Finklestein has collected her own paycheck for four years as a secretary in an advertising agency. She takes French lessons at the Alliance Française, cooks with James Beard, sculpts and Zens at The New School, and dances to rhythms at the YMHA. On Her Own in the city, Ellen treats herself with care, as though her parents lurked right behind the folding doors to her cramped galley kitchen.

"There are certain things I expect from men I date," Ellen says primly. Her demeanor is that of a proper Jewish girl (though she has had more than a few affairs over the past three years). Ellen's parents might not applaud her going to bed with different men, but they would cheer her high standards for how her escorts treat her. "I want my date to come over and pick me up. Even if we're only going to spend the evening at his place, he should show up for our date at my door. I dropped one guy because he made me take a cab over to his apartment. He paid for the cab, but that wasn't the point. I like to be treated properly." Proper treatment also includes where to go on a date. "My best date in the last year was La Caravelle." Ellen refuses to go to singles bars because the men there are not "classy" enough. Grossinger's? "Are you kidding?" Her vacations are spent at various "Club Meds" (Club Mediterranée), international resorts with a more "cosmopolitan" (to quote Ellen) clientele. An habitué of Bloomingdale's, Ellen haunts the store on Saturday mornings. Bloomingdale's is apparently the seventies version of Grossinger's. Lined up around the first floor makeup counters, packed into the gourmet food shop, crowding the escalators, is the best-dressed group of single New Yorkers anyone is likely to encounter in one place. Saturday is the time for grand rounds, to meet, mix and mingle over baskets of breads, racks of unisex handbags or inside stunning model rooms. "Somehow getting picked up in Bloomingdale's is all right," according to Ellen's standards. "It's as good as meeting someone in the Museum of Modern Art sculpture garden. It's like you have this thing about good quality in common. Besides, every well-raised Jewish Prince shops in Bloomie's."

Cheerful, round-faced Ellen, with her razor-cut short hair and carefully matched pastel pink pants outfit, is an affable expert. Who taught her everything she knows? Her parents, Ellen confides. They always wanted her to have good things, the best clothes, schools, apartment, husband. Why, at age nine, Ellen says, she had already selected steak béarnaise as her favorite food. What can anyone do with someone trained like that? No wonder Ellen goes to La Caravelle and the rest of us end up with Colonel Sanders. Who is going to have the nerve to start denying her anything at this late date?

Certainly the Jewish Prince is not going to say no. Despite all Portnoyed protests to the contrary, men who date the Ellens of this world do not choose them because of their simple tastes. On the contrary, a Jewish Prince may need a Jewish Princess as badly as she needs him. "My princess? I love her," says one well-trained prince. "She calls me up, says we must learn to play backgammon. What's backgammon, I ask her. It's the new, in thing to do, she tells me. We go to the fanciest restaurants, ones where a Spanish maître d' squirts wine in your mouth from twenty feet away and doesn't miss. Expensive tastes? You wanna see my American Express and Diner's Club bills? If we go to a deli, it has to be the best deli. We have to shop in stores where Jackie Onassis shops."

But it's Baccarat crystal clear what makes the Jewish Prince such an easy mark for the Jewish Princess. Taught by his mother, a former Jewish Princess herself, to treat young Jewish ladies in a manner befitting their status, he is raised to be reverent. An Atlanta Jewish Prince recalled his first date with a princess: "We were about to step out the door, just going for some hamburgers or something, but I felt as though the girl's family had handed over to me something infinitely precious, very valuable. I felt such an enormous responsibility. I mean God forbid, she might get scratched or something." Years of experience dating Jewish girls only confirms the prince's inbred instincts. Ari Goldman, twenty-four-year-old Jewish Prince, attractive ("adorable" the princesses say), kosher, recent graduate of the Columbia Journalism School, says he is "conditioned." "I know what to do. They expect a lot coming to them. I'd say a lot of princesses don't even say thanks for an evening out. But you do it anyway. You get dressed up, first time you go to theater. It costs you a bundle but you do go for drinks or something, too. It can be a pain in the ass. But it's all part of the motions you go through and you're raised that way. After a while if you're going out with other girls who wear jeans all the time, you begin to miss putting on a jacket and tie and going someplace nice. It's a very painful thing to admit, but you come to realize that you might want a princess."

Not only does a prince treat the princess like fragile china, he also listens to her suggestions, which can be anything but delicate. Cut your hair, get rid of that moustache, let your sideburns grow a little, change your tie. One Great Neck princess insisted that her fiancé have "just a little plastic surgery" on a small childhood scar on his chin. Into the hospital he went and out he came, scarless and perfect, to her exact specifications.

Another prince says his advice to anyone dating a Jewish Princess is "never, never go shopping with her. Once they gotcha, then they put the clamps down." He groans, but he goes every week for the shopping tour. "How about a new pair of slacks? I saw some great ones and I'll go with you to pick them out," she says. Locked inside the confines of the store's three-way mirror, he is handed select things to try on. "Put this jacket on, just try it," she says. "But I don't like it," he frowns. "But just try it on. Maybe you'll like it if you try it on." He tries it on. The jacket is much louder than the more conservative Brooks Brothers image the prince has cultivated but ten minutes later out comes his charge card and into a box goes the checked blazer. Why? "To please her, to make her happy." And, it also seems, to shut her up.

But the mating madness goes on, even with liberated princess Lynn, who envisioned herself as the one true free spirit ever born and raised in the Bronx. Over her parents' objections, she dropped out of Vassar College, and spent a year hitchhiking and backpacking across the United States. She worked as a waitress in Illinois, and a maid in Colorado ("I knew how to be a maid because I always watched ours," Lynn said). Her final three months away from home were spent on a commune in New Mexico. Very unprincesslike behavior, it seems.

After Lynn returned home to the Bronx to live with her parents, she met and dated a young man from Brooklyn. One night, at his apartment, the boy said he was tired of schlepping her home. Would she stay over? Liberated Lynn spent an hour searching her soul. After a year on the road, doing what she pleased away from home, Lynn was afraid of a direct confrontation with Momma and Poppa. A discussion of The Problem then took place.

He: "It's almost two hours by subway to get you home."

She: "But they're my parents, you know. They've given me everything."

Finally, she decided to call home. Her father picked up the phone. "I'm staying over with Alan in Brooklyn tonight," she told him. "I just want you to have the number in case you need me." She hung up quickly. Three minutes later the phone rang. It was her mother.

"Your father and I would prefer it if you came home tonight." Home she went.

Lynn, a Jewish Princess, is obedient. She listens. Another side of the Jewish Princess is that she is the world's first and foremost Good Girl. That makes it difficult these days, what with sexual freedom trumpeted by *Cosmopolitan*, Dinah Shore and Dr. Rubin. What's a nice

Jewish Princess to do? On the one hand, there are her parents' careful instructions and on the other, dire prophecies of doom. In the end, the perennial Jewish vestal virgin may succumb to the 1970's siren song of Sex. But the image of Good Girl pursues her even between the sheets. Have you heard the joke about the Jewish nymphomaniac? Once a month.

5

THE PRINCESS IN BED

As the Woody Allen story supposedly goes, he met his ex-wife one day and asked her if she'd like to go to bed with him, for old times' sake. "Over my dead body," she answered. "Why not?" he replied. "Isn't that the way we always used to do it?"

At heart, a Jewish Princess represents the culmination of the do's and don'ts she learns as she grows up female in a Jewish household.

The Jewish Princess Major No-Nos

1) Never go on any trip longer than twelve hours without checking in with your mother. She worries.

2) Never sit on a public toilet seat without putting paper down on it. Carry your own Kleenex in case they only provide those stingy little squares of wax paper.

3) Do not ride in Volkswagens, foreign sports cars or any make of convertible. They're dangerous.

4) Take cabs. In a cash emergency, borrow a buck for

the trip from the doorman. Next best alternative? The bus. Never, if possible, ride the subways and God forbid, you should never even dream of hitching.

5) Never wear your eyeglasses when there is the possibility of a nice single Jewish guy seeing you. And do not squint, it makes wrinkles.

The Jewish Princess Essential Musts

1) Sunday is Family Day and all other plans are canceled. See your mother and Live. If you have to travel more than two hours and you live alone, bring your laundry.

2) Let your parents pay you back for anything. You bring a challah to Momma for Friday night dinner? It cost seventy-five cents? You're thirty-three years old? Take the money. You know your father will have a heart attack if you do not.

3) Anywhere you go, Bring Something. Dinner parties? Housewarmings? Baby visiting? Relative-hopping? Simchas Torah? Passover Seder? You care enough to bring the very best wine, flowers, candy, cake, cookies, tiny little scented soaps, guest towels, chocolate matzo, kosher salami, Barricini licorice all sorts, sour balls for the elderly (Schrafft's, naturally). Empty-handed is out. You have been trained.

4) Let someone else do it. Your skirts are hemmed by a good tailor, your blouses ironed by a French hand laundry, your floors are waxed by a home care firm, your large parties (anything over dinner for eight or cocktails

for ten) are catered. Why should you have to work so hard?

5) Charge everything. Jewish Princesses never, ever carry cash. If you have no credit cards of your own, charge it to your mother.

What major topic is missing in this accounting? You guessed it. Sex.

A Jewish Princess receives no straight party line on sex. Either she learns about the subject from the dirty kids on the block or she has to settle for parental nuances filtered through a veil of silence.

Proof that Jewish Princesses face many uncertainties and confusions coping with the delicate matter of sex appears irrefutable. Hundreds upon thousands of Jewish men mix, mingle and even marry the dreaded species of shiksa simply because they think shiksas are free of all that sexual mishigoss. Nice Jewish boys flee the princess en masse in an effort to escape her uptight heritage. A Jewish Princess, to them, is Miss Matzo Ball, Lady Twin Beds, the girl who says "Don't touch." And today who wants to be stuck with such an unliberated partner?

So princes run to the golden goyish girls whom they fancy as free spirits, blond-haired sirens who lure them onto the rocks of intermarriage. What is wrong with Jewish girls is reflected in what Jewish men think is so right with the goyim:

"They have blond hair. They have blue eyes. They are always cuter. And they have a sense of ease, they aren't so anxious," says one Mark Cross prince.

Another young man gets misty over his past rolls in the unkosher hay: "I remember one who was terrific. She was so leggy. Another had a golden mane, and a chin. Extraordinary! I never saw a Jewish girl with a real chin."

Jewish men (despite endless years of Hebrew school, bar mitzvahs, carefully supervised kosher upbringings and occasional attacks of Zionism), are irresistibly drawn to non-Jewish women. It is an addiction. Hopelessly, helplessly, the princes line up to confess that they cannot rid themselves of the fantasies: Catherine Deneuve, Marilyn Monroe, Swedish airline stewardesses, apple-cheeked Midwestern farm girls. "The attraction," says one spaced-out soul, "is definitely sexual, the ultimate, fantastic, hallucinatory voyage."

A trip to bed with a Jewish Princess fails to garner the same "X" rating as the gentile pleasure cruise. And each Jewish Prince who stepped forward to report problems with a princess in bed, diagnosed the sexual trouble as only one person's failure: Hers.

Where did the Jewish Princess get her reputation? Partially, the stereotype arose from the detailed reports about the games men must play in order to coax poor, hung up princesses into going all the way. The modern-day Homers who spread these legends are something like Mitchell Freedman, an experienced bachelor of twenty-eight who frequents the East Side Manhattan singles scene. Mitchell describes his forays into Jewish Princess territory as something akin to General Patton's troop movements.

"Going to bed with a princess is something an Arab

shouldn't experience," says Mitchell as he downs a martini at a Third Avenue bar.

What's the big megillah?

"We go to bed, we make it, and she has such guilt," goes Mitchell's Complaint. "I'm not guilty, why should I be? I'm fairly truthful. I'll say to her, 'You enjoyed it, I enjoyed it, what's bad?' But a Jewish Princess won't allow herself to enjoy it. Now, take my girlfriend from Denmark. She wouldn't give me any of that crap."

Can we believe this witness? Certainly Mitchell is no acne-faced, grubby-looking kid. He is a man-about-town circa 1975, complete with a tailored Paul Stuart suit, tinted aviator glasses, Jackie Rogers-coiffed hair and a copy of the *Wall Street Journal*. In other words, a real catch, a single Jewish Princess' dream. But to hear him talk, he apparently does not dream about the princess. And his descriptions bring back some element of the furtive fifties, a memory of scrambling in the back seat of a car at a drive-in. To Mitchell, the Jewish Princess is a sexual throwback to an earlier time, and he treats her in precisely that fashion.

"With a princess, the whole idea of going to bed with a man, especially not a husband, is forbidden from Day One," Mitchell states with great authority.

How, then, does one seduce a JP?

"Well, the Jewish Princess has to be raped. She can't just want to get into bed. I have to work on her. She just lies there. First I feel her chest. 'Take your hand away,' she says. But I tell her, 'Anything wrong with me touching your hand? You like holding hands.' She says no. So I move my hand up her sleeve. 'Nothing wrong with me touching your sweater, is there?' Then I zero in. I tell her, 'I assume you're wearing a bra. That's even more protection over your skin.' I go for her tits then, with my hand. 'There, that's the same skin as on your hand but protected by the sweater and the bra!'"

His smile is triumphant. "There may be more struggle with the hand, minor skirmishing, but once it's on her tit, you're home free. A more direct approach, like going for the crotch, shocks them."

Mitchell the swinger demands perfection in his women. A true Jewish male chauvinist, his idea of the ideal mate is a girl who believes in free love and freshly squeezed orange juice every morning. In his experience, he has found the Jewish Princess to be a sexual lost cause. Her hang-ups are "hopeless," says he.

But talking with a straighter, unswingy Jewish bachelor reveals that not all of Mitchell's talk is sour Manischewitz grapes. Square guys, too, find the Jewish Princess a bit troubled and say that all of the sweat expended in finally getting her into bed is terribly unsexy.

One enchanted evening, Stanley Seligmann wined and dined a Chicago Princess and then took her home to his little bachelor flat with the foldout Castro Convertible. Innocent, accommodating Stanley, with his slides from Israel, his collection of Bernard Malamud and Elie Wiesel novels, and his penny loafers, discovered that Miss Lake Shore Drive was a liberated lady, so she said.

"I want to do anything, try anything," she told a surprised Stanley.

Stanley the nebbish was not about to "go for the crotch"

or anything quite so drastic. In fact, as politely as if asking her if she wanted a chocolate-covered mint, he said, "How do you want to do it? On top, on a club chair (with a towel to protect the slip cover), on the floor, or good old Missionary style? What would you like to do?"

The girl hesitated a good while, then replied, "Anything you want, you decide."

"Okay," said Stanley, "let's do it on the floor."

"I don't want to do that," she said, pouting.

"How about in the chair?"

"No," said she, again.

"Then why did you bother to ask me to pick out a position in the first place?" asked frustrated Stanley, quite annoyed.

"I don't know," she said truthfully, "but you decide."

The couple finally did make it, I was led to believe, but Stanley never said exactly where.

In addition to these true-to-life episodes in the Perils of Propositioning Princesses, there are certain general attitudes about the princess floating around among Jewish men that can be summed up simply as "She lacks SA." SA, or Sex Appeal, is what makes our society run these days, the push behind the fascination with youthful clothes, exercise, makeup, cremes, lighteners and conditioners. And though the Jewish Princess follows the dictates of fashion very faithfully, she cannot seem to shake the reputation that she is a terrific prude and rather too forbiddingly smart and ballsy to be anyone's true sex object.

Herewith, an illustration of "The Prejudiced, Anti-Princess Sex Bias of the Jewish Male":

When brilliant, beautiful Jewish Princess law student Sandra joined a prestigious Jewish law firm as a summer intern, she was convinced all the men in the office were secretly lusting for her body. It would have to be secretly, because after six weeks of work, no one in that high-powered, monied firm made even a furtive pass. Surprised by the lack of interest, Sandra mentioned the situation to friend and fellow law student Gary.

"How come," she said, "they chase after the gentile secretaries and stenos and completely ignore me?"

"Ah hah, my dear," Gary sagely replied. "You are a Jewish girl and no one thinks a smart lady like you is interested in screwing around."

To prove his point, Gary planned a little experiment to take place the day of a posh party to be given by the firm at a Darien estate. He escorted Sandra to the affair disguised in a Salvation Army sport jacket, sporting a three day's growth of beard and talking in his best blue-collar accent. Picking Sandra up on party day in a battered Buick, he said, "I yam your date, a cabbie from da Bronx."

Parking hard by the Mercedes and Cadillacs on the circular graveled drive, Gary and Sandy headed for the party, spread out around the perimeter of a gorgeous, free-form swimming pool. Bartenders presided over collections of crystal and sterling silver equipment, polite waiters passed trays of Sunday afternoon country hors d'oeuvres, and the crowd, dressed in their casual, Gucci and Pucci best, stood in small groups and exchanged cocktail chatter.

The couple's entrance caused a mild stir which

increased when Gary ordered a beer and tilted the bottle to his mouth. No one could quite comprehend this curious pairing of brains and Bronxese.

A small crowd of courteous but curious attorneys soon surrounded Gary. "What do you do for a living?" they inquired.

"Drive a cab midtown," he replied, taking another swig of beer.

"Have you been going out with Sandra for long?" another lawyer queried.

"Couple of months. And lemmie tell youse, she is some terrific piece of ass," Gary said loudly.

The lawyers shot raised-eyebrow looks at one another and glanced around to see if their wives had heard. Then they continued their cross-examination. "But you must know," said one, "that Sandra is one of our most brilliant and promising trainees?"

"That's okay for youse, but boy, get her into bed and she is somethin' else. That's some great broad you have there," Gary told them.

Everyone turned to stare at Sandra, their neat little world of stereotypes shaken. Why, she was the aggressive, brainy Jewish girl. What would she be doing putting out in bed for this shlump, going out just for sex? The idea boggled their orderly, legal brains. Consider the possibilities: they had Jewish wives, lovely homes, beautiful children and an occasional "hot" shiksa on the side. But had they ever heard of a hot Jewish Princess on the side?

Just then, a friend of Gary's family came over and recognized him under his grungy disguise. "How's law school?" he asked Gary. And the lawyers laughed in relief, glad it was all just a little joke.

But we who know better realize that Jewish Princess sex myths do not die in laughter. They persist, because Jewish men serve as their most prominent enforcers. And some of the strength of the stereotype has to do with a Jewish male's familiarity with the Jewish heritage and its traditional taboos against sex. Jewish women endured centuries of religious rigmarole which included trips to a mikva (ritual bath) seven days following menstruation, a mathematical calculation for cleanliness which made Jewish wives available to their husbands for sex about two weeks of every month. The week after her period ended, the Jewish bride ran off to the bath, to be dunked into the pool three times and pronounced "kosher" like some poor, bloodless, rabbinically approved chicken in the marketplace. Eagerly heading for home, she announced her newly blessed availability to her mate by handing him some object, since even passing a husband a fork or spoon before the bath was verboten. After he got the spoon (and the message), sex could proceed on schedule, which meant at night. Foreplay was a prayer. A quick brocha, and everything was ready to go. The whole procedure was apparently designed to ensure procreation, no wasting of a single fertile moment. But cleanliness, just as the koshering of meat involves proper removal of all blood, was as important as fertility. And above all, no distractions from women were tolerated, neither hair (matrons' heads were shaved), nor sleeveless clothes, nor even singing. Sexy women were sacrilegious.

Today, the mikva is gone but the memory must linger on in the aura of embarrassment and the perpetuation of sexual ignorance that pervades many Jewish homes. Mothers today may still simply ignore the subject, or spill out too much too soon—another form of embarrassment. Communication, what little there is, is accomplished by nuance and inflection. Impossible as it is to imagine a Jewish mother being subtle, subtle she is about sex. She may give her daughter a printed manual published by the Modess people (which informs drugstore buyers that the trade name rhymes with "Oh Yes," an instruction obviously aimed at the more brazen goyim), and send her off to see a Walt Disney-style film on menstruation with animated ovaries and eggs. So where do Jewish girls learn where the Tampax goes? Literature and helpful friends, but she has to be oh so careful not to touch herself down there. Morals? Simple. Daughters are told repeatedly to be "good girls," and after hearing that ten times or more a day, they come to associate "good" with "no."

If Jewish mothers take it upon themselves to break the silence, they may often do more harm than good. They have a tendency to react to their own straight-laced upbringings by Telling All to their little daughters (and sons) much too early. The end result is just about the same as in the terribly silent households: The little princess grows up to be quite a confused young woman.

When Karen Fishman, a twenty-year-old student at Sarah Lawrence, was all of five years old, she was taken on a jaunt up to a lakeside resort. She and her mother and grandmother spent a week away from the city at a small cottage. One day, Karen ran home to her mother to ask her all about a grand new expression she just picked up from a little playmate: "What does 'knocked up' mean, Mommy?"

Mommy, Mildred Fishman, faced her Moment of Truth and opted for the honest approach. Now, she figured, was as good a time as any to tell Karen the most embarrassing story ever told. So sitting her small daughter on her lap and taking a deep breath, she plunged in: "During every month, a woman ovulates once, producing an egg which, if fertilized by a male sperm, starts to subdivide into hundreds of cells. The fetus, which is what the early stage is called, develops in the womb, surrounded by the placenta which nourishes it and is tied by the umbilical cord to the woman."

Karen, lulled by the sound of her mother's voice, stuck her thumb into her mouth. Just then, Momma Mildred heard the sound of another voice, coming from the front of the house, a voice chanting something over and over again, angrily, in Yiddish. Another generation to be heard from: Grandma. Mildred marched out to the porch and found her mother seated on a rocking chair, pushing it back and forth with a tapping foot, her face a flaming red. The translation of Grandma's chant? "How appalling it is that such a discussion can take place between a mother and a little child." Closing the front door, Mildred went back in to Karen determined to finish her lecture. But by this time, little Karen was fast asleep in the chair. Later, when Mildred asked her daughter if she wanted to hear some more, Karen grinned and said, "Oh, yes, Mommy. Talk more, so fast and funny!"

Grandma, insufferably silent with daughter Mildred during her upbringing, strictly disapproved of Mildred saying a word to her granddaughter. And poor Mildred, crushed by her bungled attempt at the summer cottage, was hard-pressed to pick up the thread of the subject again. The end result is found in the person of Karen, who is currently living with her boyfriend. And this boyfriend, like all of Karen's friends and each of her previous involvements, is (you guessed it) not Jewish.

All of this generational mishigoss suggests that though many families have a difficult time communicating, when it comes to sex talk, the Jewish family may have set some kind of nonrecord. No one knows what to do (except Karen, and her solution is to avoid other meshuggener Jewish kids).

To be fair, many non-Jewish girls have their own hang-ups (note the proliferation of all the recent articles on "How to Have a Successful Orgasm"), but Jewish Princesses treat their sex problems with their own special style. They lead double lives, as Jewish Princess Number One, the demure girl Mom and Dad know who sleeps in her own bed, alone, and Jewish Princess Number Two, the same person who juggles two affairs simultaneously. Thus, the princess may act the cold fish for her parents while attempting to show skeptical Jewish guys she is some hot tomato. But when the two images clash, some Keystone Cops antics ensue.

Joyce Katz, a Scarsdale girl in her late twenties, claims to be truly liberated. At least, she is liberated in her own apartment, away from her family. At home she is still vestal virgin Joyce.

"Oh, come on," Joyce says, shaking her shaggy mop of hair when princess sex problems are mentioned. "Jewish girls may just talk about their hang-ups more than anyone. But we're really not that repressed at all. I've always done what I've wanted to do."

Really, Joyce?

Stage one in her bachelor girl's setup was to rent her own apartment. Stage two was to move in with her boyfriend. Stage three was to make it back to her own place before her mother's eight A.M. daily phone call. And as if that weren't bad enough, things got worse when her sister visited town and went to see her own boyfriend every night. Then two young women made the early morning mad dash back together, to talk soothingly to Momma about having just stepped out of the shower and *that's* why I'm late for the phone call.

All of this careful planning is designed to protect an overprotective momma. Mrs. Katz was so careful with her girls that they never learned anything they wanted to know about you know what at home. Joyce says she received a basic sex education from a friend's copy of *Peyton Place* and the illustrated anatomy section of the *Encyclopaedia Britannica* in the library. Mrs. Katz's reticence and shrinking violet approach to the subject leads her daughters and husband to believe that even today, with her children fully grown, she must be protected from knowing anything. At a Sunday afternoon cookout, Mr. Katz decided to joke with his wife and looked up at her over the sizzling steaks to ask, "How does it feel to have two daughters shacking up?" Poor Momma paled, turned on her heel and fled into the house "to get the salad dressing."

The same scenes happen again and again as princesses take enormous pains to protect their families. Jewish women are not content merely to avoid the subject of sex around their mothers and fathers, they work hard at reassurance. So hard, in fact, that a perennial Jewish momma's gift to the bride (who probably lived with her intended for a year previous) is a copy of *Love Without Fear* and a tube of K-Y Jelly.

Much of a princess' reputation for being uptight comes from these ritual bows to the family rather than her actual behavior in bed. A case in point occurred in Great Neck, on the occasion of a New Year's Eve celebration attended by a crowd of young suburban Jews. The party, held in a starkly modern house complete with quadraphonic piped-in music and water beds, was as dull as any suburban eggnog affair. Despite ritual pot smoking and Alice Toklas brownie gobbling, stifled yawns swept the room. One man's date left forty-five minutes before midnight, sleepy and disgusted. The guy stayed on, trying to get adequately stoned and perhaps pick up another date. When the party began to break up at one thirty A.M., he went to get his coat and noticed a young woman off in a corner, staring rather openly at him. She was clad in silver lamé evening pants and a bare midriff satin halter top. Staring back, he foggily tried to remember who the hell she was. Ah, yes, this was Francine, his best friend's date and acting hostess for the evening. Soon everyone had left except for the happy threesome of Francine, the host, and our stoned friend.

97

Somehow, they ended up making waves on a water bed, a perfect Great Neck trio, two Jewish Princes and a raving Jewish Princess (whose sexual behavior, it must be added, was reportedly "quite wild" and extremely unprincesslike, the men said).

Nevertheless, at four A.M. Francine suddenly sat bolt upright in bed, reached for the phone and began to dial. Hey, what's happening, the guys wanted to know. "I have to call my mother," said Francine. "I have to tell her I'm having such a good time at this party that I'm not coming home."

Francine's Pavlovian reaction proved once again how well a Jewish Princess is trained. Which is precisely why they have difficulty being decisive about premarital sex. No one tells them directly not to do it. There are no hard-and-fast rules for them to follow in this tricky area. In fact, only one Jewish Princess recalled any direct pronouncement against sex from her mother and it dealt more concretely with the girl dating a Christian than with her carnal behavior. "You go out with a shaygets," said the momma, "and someday you'll wind up in bed with a crucifix hanging over your head."

With all of the sex myths and stereotypes abounding on the subject of the Jewish Princess, it's a wonder every Jewish man and woman don't run out and intermarry, if only to avoid being confronted with all of this nonsense every time they decide they want to get laid. But crosses and little blond-haired children aside, Jewish Princes do marry Jewish Princesses, simply because they are born and bred to do so. Jewish girls are taught that Jewish boys will make excellent husbands: nondrinkers who will earn lots of money and be warm, loving daddies. Jewish boys are instructed to appreciate the finer points of a Jewish wife: her chopped liver almost as good as Momma's, her stylish appearance and her beautiful taste in china and crystal. Certainly, the match is made in heaven, if only because it makes everyone's parents so happy (and because anxious Jewish mommas and poppas think that marrying a Jew means their child is eternally saved from the shame of marrying a gentile).

The act of sex is thus only a prelude to the future march down the aisle. Being a sensuous lover is not as important as being marriageable. A Jewish Princess is after Her Man and if she has to go to bed with him, she'll go to bed with him.

And thus the old story, what's the easiest way to get a Jewish girl to stop screwing? Marry her.

6

THE PERFECT PRINCESS

> She looketh well to the ways of her household, And eateth
> not the bread of idleness.
> > —The Jewish wife, according to Proverbs

Meet Barbara. She and her-husband-the-lawyer live in a
suburb of New York, in a five-room apartment with a
terrace overlooking the Hudson River. Their neighborhood is not ritzy, but there are signs of obvious wealth. A
quick car count in the parking garage brings the total of
four-door sedans to at least twice the number of VWs. And
the ladies who stand on the corner and wait for the
Express Bus to Manhattan clutch lilac-sprigged Bonwit's
bags and tiny Tiffany paper totes, undoubtedly culled
from their stellar collection of status shopping bags.

Barbara's apartment is on the sixteenth floor, with a
living room view of the Hudson (which looks clean from
up on high) and the green Jersey Palisades. However, we
looked at the river only after Barbara raised the fluted,
lacy white shades and pulled aside the printed drapes.
Bright sunshine, I am crisply informed, fades carpets.

Barbara's apartment is smothered in plush, shaggy, multicolored carpeting, wall-to-wall and room-to-room, even into the bathrooms, walk-in closets and onto the terrace. Barbara and the decorator have "conceived" and executed the apartment in a conservative yet modern style, with velvet-covered furniture in buttery beiges or burnt golds, coordinated wallpaper and loads of needlepoint pillows. It's all there: carefully arranged magazines fanned out on the glass coffee table in the den (*Vogue, Harper's Bazaar, Time, Newsweek* and *Forbes*), carved handles on every doorknob, and distinctly different plates on each and every light switch.

First stop on the private house tour was Barbara's special place, her dressing room. Once a mere box of a hallway between boudoir and bath, now it is transformed into a tiny Hall of Mirrors backed by special lighting that can be switched on to "simulate daylight," I am told. Before the mirrors stands a small shrine to beauty, a dressing table groaning under the load of Clinique cosmetics, facial masks, skin toners, astringents, cleansers and creams. Center stage, a bottle of Joy, highlight of the collection. Trotting back into the bedroom, which featured a genuine fur bedspread (not an endangered species mind you, but minks' tails, which Barbara was "lucky" to get through a wholesaler), Barbara led me immediately to her armoire, with its made-to-order, built-in interior dividers. Inside, a burglar's paradise, a repository of the lady's crown jewels, stashed in special jewelry cases designed to line everything up in a neat processional. Earrings, dozens of pairs, bracelets, chains, beads, and "dinner rings." I am then steered over to pride and joy number two, a chrome and steel étagère which holds an assortment of crystal objects that I am told in breathy awe, are "Laliques."

Not to be missed on the schlep through the house is the kitchen. One must see the set of shining electrical appliances that puts Hammacher Schlemmer to shame: grinders, pulverizers, baconers, roasters, grillers, mashers and crushers. I was then introduced to Dolores, the maid, who makes "terrific crêpes and marvelous Lobster Newburg."

Other hidden treasures in this model flat were hubby's collection of fine wines, methodically stacked in its own cool, dark, compartment built into a corner of an extra closet. And, finally, last stop, the lady's linens. Barbara opened the closet door and the moment was akin to the premiere unfolding of NBC's color peacock. A barrage of color jumped out at the eye, piles of bright Yves St. Laurent towels, coordinated sets of Vera and Bill Blass sheets and pillow cases. I estimated the linen was enough for three households and all of it sat in state, freshly pressed, neatly stacked on wall-papered shelves scented with a light touch of lemon sachet.

Although Barbara does not work, she has hardly a moment to spare. Most of her week consists of a variety of trips into "the city," where she meets friends for lunch and shopping or visits her mother, for more lunches and shopping. Barbara also takes museum courses; her latest recently completed lecture series was, "Adventures in Flemish and Dutch Masterpieces of the Late 16th

Century." Barbara said she missed only three lectures, two when she went to Barbados and one when she had matinee tickets with Mother. Once a week she has her hair done and once a month her eyelashes individually applied. A few times a year she adds leg waxing, too. Twice a week, she plays tennis in the morning at a local club with three friends and also does volunteer work for two charities, MS and CP. Every weekend, Barbara entertains or is entertained, and religiously, she has her mother over "without fail" on Sundays. Often she gives a little brunch then, replacing those "boring bagels and lox" menus with a small quiche and perhaps black bread and whitefish. There are no current movies Judith Crist raves about that Barbara has not seen nor any Broadway show that got a blessing from Clive Barnes that the couple has not watched from mid-orchestra. Plus, of course, the two are permanently in attendance at all of the Knicks and Rangers home games. With what little time remains, Barbara and husband work with an architect on plans for the couple's new home in Westchester. How active the couple's sex life must be is anybody's guess; the only hint on the subject is Barbara's remark that she went off the Pill because it made her gain weight, that she disdains a diaphragm because of the mess and dislikes condoms because they're really very ugly. That leaves foam or rhythm, but Barbara carries the discussion no further.

Barbara is twenty-three. Her husband is twenty-five. The were married a year and a half ago. Barbara says she is content, secure and happily mated. A Perfect Princess: adorned with complete Royal Copenhagen service for twelve, a Braun juice extractor, and three extension phones (one princess, one push-button, one wall phone with fifty-foot extension cord), living in a world where everything is precisely the way she wants it, where she never sleeps on the same pattern of sheets for three consecutive weeks. What's the secret? How do you learn to live like Barbara? "You have to take extremely good care of yourself."

The desire to be a Perfect Princess is as strong as any drive channeled into a career. What Barbara does is to translate the goal of "making it" into the standard she lives up to: the Most you can have of the Best. "This is how I expect to live," Barbara said. "My friends all have the same things I do. When it comes down to paying a difference of twenty-five dollars, or even a couple of hundred dollars to get exactly what I want, I don't mind. It's better than settling for something not quite right and then having to live with things that just miss. And my husband understands this. He wouldn't stop at spending the money on what he wants, so why should I?" The Perfect Princess does not settle for anything less than what she wants.

Whereas Barbara moved into a heightened stage of acquisitiveness when she married, there are those Perfect Princesses who have not waited for the ceremony. Barbara had a friend, for example, who wanted the most gorgeous diamond ring available. Was she interested in number of carats? No, size was too "tacky." She wanted a flawless gem. How did she make sure her ring would measure up? First of all, she accompanied her fiancé on all of his ring-buying expeditions. Tray after tray of twinkling rings were carted to the counter and placed before them. The girl would open up her handbag and produce her very own jeweler's eye. Screwing it into place, she picked up every single rock and gave it the once-over. The jeweler, no doubt, looked on in amazement as she sifted and winnowed his collection.

This diamond maven is an example of the Perfect Princess in action, pre-wedding. But some of her ilk do not see marriage at the end of the ring, and they become perennial fiancées. Stop and ask such a princess about the origins of all the baubles and bangles that adorn her lovely golden self, and she will provide a list of romantic encounters: "This bracelet I got when I was lavaliered. And this pin, here, the one on the right, was from when I was first engaged. My fiancé Mark and I are planning to get married next year. He's the one who gave me my diamond." As she extends her left hand, I ask myself whether that wedding will ever come off, or will she decide she needs another bracelet and cancel?

Another jewelry princess had her ex-fiancé's family heirloom engagement ring made into a pin after the couple broke up. "Why waste a good diamond?" was her rationale. But the Queen of the engagement-hopping circuit was a girl from Finch College known only as Patricia. Each time she got engaged, which was more than once during her reign, she got a bigger ring. Friends say she married the fourth ring, apparently big enough to suit her tastes. The wedding was held soon after Mr. Right presented her with her diamond by placing it into a glass of champagne. She nearly swallowed it, and reportedly said, "It looked just like an ice cube."

First comes the diamond, then immediately following, the registration of silver patterns, china and crystal. The Perfect Princess often goes ahead and selects her choice, despite the best advice of Mother, who says, "Don't pick things that are too expensive. Not everyone can afford to give you a place setting of china which goes for ninety dollars. Take something for forty dollars, so guests can afford it. Don't be like that friend of yours who registered for hand-painted things at one hundred and ten dollars a place setting!"

But even the princess with a smaller scale wedding wants the full glory of the right wedding gifts. One bride, who insisted firmly that her wedding be kept small, would not hear of a guest list larger than forty. All the same, she proceeded to sign up for Royal Copenhagen china and Baccarat crystal as though she were having two hundred. After the reception was over, she excitedly reviewed the loot and counted one lone place setting of china and four champagne glasses. Anyone dining at her home is warned, as they sip sangría, "If you break one, you're dead." Poor girl, she has to keep her dinner parties terribly intimate, if only to cart out her crystal.

But do not for a moment think that the buck stops there. Oh, no, get ready to spend thousands on the pièce de résistance. The wedding. Anyone with suitable high standards has only one proper way to get married: with Everything.

One wedding in Chicago had it all. At least, it seemed so from the sister-in-law's point of view. When a princess from Lake Shore Drive wed an up-and-coming orthopedic surgeon (much to the delight of both sides of the family, this perfect blend of money and medicine), no expense was spared. Perfection, our observer reported, costs upwards of a cool $15,000 these days, "but if it makes our daughter happy," the parents agreed, "we'll do it." Of course, Mom and Dad really mean it makes them happy, but once the whole affair is underway, no bride pouts her way through all of that glamour. As the wedding photos indicated, her mother may have been major domo, but she turned out the Star.

The curtain went up in Chicago with the invitations. "Engraved, from Tiffany's, naturally," the sister-in-law reported, noting the embossed Tiffany mark snuck beneath all of the envelope flaps. Since the wedding was held in temple and the reception followed at a chic country club, guests received a fat packet of instructions with their invitations. "You could break your arm lifting it," said our sister-in-law friend, handing over the evidence. The thick packet was printed in raised script on creamy beige paper. Each envelope was individually lettered in black ink, in Gothic script which featured formal salutations. Our informant's little boy got his own invitation addressed to "Master Eric." Inside the envelopes? Ceremony invitation ("the honour of your presence is requested"), reception invitation ("request the pleasure of your company"), map of how to get from Temple to Country Club ("left at the first Exxon station following the second traffic signal"), and RSVP cards to be mailed back (each return envelope addressed and stamped with cunning Robert Indiana-designed postage stamps that proclaim "LOVE" with that famous cockeyed "O").

"They lit the entire sanctuary with candles. They had candles at the top of the topiary trees that lined the aisle, in the center of big bunches of asparagus fern, baby's breath and apricot tulips. Long streamers of beige ribbon ran from tree-to-tree to mark off the aisle. For the chuppah, she had a white frame constructed, covered with gladiolas and greens, and baskets of more tulips, which they later used at the country club behind the band. Every man was handed a beige velvet yarmulke, to match the color scheme, and it had the bride and groom's names and date printed in gold inside."

She noted that "Here Comes the Bride" had been supplanted by something else she thinks was "Bach, but I'm not too sure." (A later check discovered it was "Trumpet Voluntary," by Purcell.) Then her fashion report : "Groom's mother, peach chiffon Bill Blass; bride's mother, coral-sequined sheath by Adele Simpson. The maid of honor, something ruffly and floral-patterned in orange tones, from Saks. She was much too young for a name designer, they were right about that. But the bride wore an Adolfo. What more can I say? Stunning. I understand she flew to New York four times for her fittings!"

The remainder of the report on the main event consisted predominantly of comparisons of numbers. The last four weddings a guest has been to had six-piece bands? "She had ten pieces, plus a guy who doubled on the accordion for the cocktail hour." And the food? At other affairs our spy recalled the usual hors d'oeuvres and a table or two of hot things. Not here. "She had, and I counted to be sure, four tables of seafood alone. There were piles of cold crab, shrimp, clams, oysters, and a man who would make hot scampi, fra diavolo, shrimps in wine, whatever you asked for, to order on the spot. Plus three tables with huge loaves of pumpernickel, lox, nova, sturgeon, which I haven't seen at a wedding in years, and bowls of tomato, onion rings and cream cheese. I could have stopped right there! And there were passed hot canapés, too, more conventional—stuffed mushrooms, some kind of quiche, tiny chicken cacciatore, and baby meatballs." As the still photographers (two) snapped photos of the guests eating, the sister-in-law also noted the details of the color scheme: matching cocktail napkins, floral arrangement, matchbook covers, and in the ladies' room, tiny soaps and guest towels (apricot and beige, and monogrammed with the newly married couple's entwined initials).

Then, to the flourish of a march played on the accordion, the guests drifted into the main room for dinner, seven courses. The sister-in-law counted each dish, too. "They had flowing champagne, not just one bottle per table, and tiny little silver dishes of sherbet between courses which my dumb cousin Larry thought was dessert, and five hours of continuous music. Even while you ate, small groups of musicians came around to play your favorite requests, if they knew them." Dinner? I was handed a menu: ambrosia of fruits ("Scooped-out cantaloupe with mixed fruit inside"), duckling in cherry sauce flambé, petite marmite ("very watery vegetable soup"), prime ribs of beef *au jus avec champignons* (giant mushroom caps), Caesar salad, Baked Alaska, and wedding cake. "There were more guests taking home doggie bags of roast beef than I counted, I'm sure. Who could eat all of that food? Plus there was a bowl of fresh fruit, held up by this little naked marble cherub, stuck in the center of each table." Throughout the meal, she noted again that everything matched the apricot and beige color scheme, from the centerpieces ("Is your birthday nearest the wedding day?" the MC howled. "If it is, then YOU take home the flowers!"), to the napkins, the doilies beneath the sherbet, the after dinner mints and the apricot fruit filling between layers of the wedding cake.

The final act is not to be missed and our reporter stayed to the bitter end to turn in her most complete version of the wedding story. Only the late-stayers, however, got to appreciate the crowning touch: the Viennese table. But this table was not just any après dinner pastry offering with a strudel or two and a pot of coffee for the road. "This girl had a bowl of fresh strawberries the size of my bathroom sink, two bowls filled with whipped cream and fresh cream, kirsch if you preferred, six Sacher tortes, three kinds of fruit and crumb pies, petits fours, and made-to-order crêpes. I almost got sick. Then I said good-bye to my parents who looked glazed over, and rolled my husband Arthur home."

A lot of young women attempt to make their weddings qualify as legends. A Great Neck ceremony was held in a temple-in-the-round, in which a dozen violinists were spaced every thirty degrees around an upstairs balcony. As the bride marched down the aisle, they sawed away in unison at the theme from *Love Story*. Another bride stood silhouetted behind a heart-shaped screen for a full three minutes until the screen lifted. Then bright spotlights followed her slow progress down the aisle on the arm of her squinting father. Unconfirmed rumor has it that a Miami bride was scheduled to make her big appearance stepping smartly out of a giant wedding cake.

Certain mishaps often become spectacular highlights of what would otherwise be rather standard affairs. At one recent ceremony, the mother of the bride (obviously pooped from having masterminded the entire production) fainted dead away right up at the altar, seconds before her son-in-law smashed the glass. By stopping everything for a good ten minutes, while her husband and the rabbi anxiously waved handkerchiefs in her face, she cinched the Upstage-the-Bride award that year. Second runner-up was a lady from Scarsdale who donned an Elizabeth Taylor wig of black Grecian curls and a dress cut down to her navel (or to her "pupik" as the guests whispered), exposing uplifted chest and neatly removing all eyes from her demure daughter swathed to the neck in white Alençon lace.

But after the ball is over, the princess bursts into her most perfect bloom, astonishing husband, friends, and sometimes even parents who claim they had no idea she was so "organized." She stalks through her new territory, the shops, the stores, the showrooms, and wreaks mayhem with the salespeople in an effort to bring order to her own life. One goggle-eyed girl described the metamorphosis of her ex-best friend Laura, "a regular Lord & Taylor girl who married and immediately became keeper of the manse. Suddenly she had this new take-charge thing going. For a girl who couldn't keep filing straight in an office, she's incredible, arranging caterers, trips to Palm Beach, building shelves for all the knickknacks in her living room. She lives in D.C. now, and the one time I went to visit her, we spent the weekend going from the hairdresser's in Georgetown to the French bakery to the furriers to pick out pelts for her new fur coat. I saw no sights, not even the White House, but I went to Garfinckel's, three times!"

Single, the Princess is unfulfilled, untried. Married she reorganizes herself, cutting her long, straight, ironed hair into a Sassoon geometric style, plucking her eyebrows thin, discarding her old work clothes of pants and sweaters for the simplest belted shirtwaists, worn with only a smattering of swinging gold chains. Her loopy gold earrings are swapped for tiny diamond and pearl buttons. What was her filing job compared with arranging cocktails for fifty? To quiche or not to quiche, that is Laura's decision now. And she loves it. Despite the grueling competition from the other Jewish Princesses, anxious to get the same caterers or upholsterers, the Perfect Princess shtick can be fun.

Shopping? Anything qualifies for an expedition, from a can of Comet to a Waring blender. As Laura and her friend traveled back to Garfinckel's for the third time that day, Laura gushed, "I can't wait until you get married. It'll open up a whole new world of shopping for you."

The princess' shopping activities are given a shape and a

113

purpose by her major, time-consuming effort, decorating. Everything must be done with infinite care. In fact, the act of decorating is more important than the finished product, which puts the princess into a continuous state of Decoratus Interruptus. As soon as she finishes one room, she moves to the next. By the time the whole house is done, she is back to redo the first room because its original gestalt bears no resemblance to the rest of the house.

Does this mean a Jewish Princess has a subliminal desire to be a decorator? "Oh no," said one lady diligently plowing through the wallpaper books at a chic Madison Avenue shop. "I went to decorating school, but spending other people's money is no fun."

The decorating princess uses a decorator, often her mother's, since everyone knows a good decorator is hard to find. Big names are unnecessary; Uncle Harold's nephew is as good as Sister Parish. How come? Decorators do not provide a princess with social cachet; they give her access. Their cards open the doors to the maximum number of furniture, carpeting, wallpaper and bathroom accessory stores imaginable.

Margi (pronounced with a hard "g," her Margie days ended with high school), is currently in the midst of doing her apartment in San Francisco. A tiny little thing, just a bit over five feet tall, Margi goes faithfully, accompanied by her decorator (whose name she conceals as Top Secret), on daily rounds of the shops and boutiques. She returns home at night, wilting like an unwatered plant, her pants suit dusty and her long pony tail dragging, laden with armloads of fabric swatches, catalogues, drawings and chunks of carpet. After a quick shower, she changes into a halter-necked hostess gown to receive friends for dinner (everyone will sit on folding chairs around her old kitchen table). Her standard greeting at the door varies, but any line is a dead giveaway as to what is in store for the evening. Flinging open the door, she bestows lavish hugs and kisses and tells her guests, "I hope you'll forgive the way everything looks, I'm in the middle of decorating." Or, "Of course, the place isn't finished yet." Or, "You'll have to just get a general idea of what I'm trying to do." Or, for a little variation, "Guess what! I've just started to redecorate."

Margi entertains her guests with cocktails, smoked oysters, and swatches of fabric flung over the couch "to get the effect," stories of pushy Barca-lounger salesmen, and quick forays into the bathroom to study experimental dabs of various color paints.

Then after dinner, with coffee and dessert, Margi presses her company into distinguished service. "Want to help choose?" she says, her eager brown eyes widening. Tiny little Margi runs into the bedroom and comes staggering out with an armload of wallpaper rolls. Fighting off her husband's help, she proudly unfurls her trophies for the audience of friends. "For the guest bathroom," she announces. "Now, everyone who likes the silver-shiny paper, raise their hands. Good. Now the Peter Max flowers with the coordinated shower curtain. Terrific. No one likes the latticed bamboo effect with the peacocks?" Her face falls. Apparently, Margi prefers the peacocks. Still, she is resilient and bounces back by saying that next

Sunday, she will show them all to her in-laws. Everyone wishes her good luck.

On the other hand, let us give credit where credit is due, and it isn't just on the furniture bills. The Perfect Princess can do a very nice job of fixing up her home. Gone are the days when she decorated in a style fondly known as Bronx Renaissance. That era was characterized by a knee-high, wrought-iron fence enclosing the living room, a mix of French Provincial and heavy Spanish in the bedroom, a twinkly cascade of crystal chandeliers overhead in every room, and a set of framed reproductions of Greek and Roman ruin scenes. In contrast, regardez the apartment of a Cedarhurst, Long Island, couple. Randy Weinstein, twenty-five, a school teacher and part-time guidance counselor, and husband Stephen, twenty-seven, in real estate, live on the second floor of a comfortable garden apartment. Randy, pregnant, just slightly showing, and into maternity clothes already, is planning diligently how to make the den into a nursery and still utilize some of her chrome and steel furnishings. (Anyone like to see a coffee table turned into a bassinet stand?) The apartment is four rooms, with a tiny terrace.

Though the Weinstein flat is small, each of its rooms is "done." Randy has created a look in which the infinitesimal object is more important than the large pieces. This style is known as the "Correct Chatchke Effect." For example, Randy's couch may not be the most expensive, but it is covered in a costly, print fabric in splashy modern design. The tones in that fabric perfectly match the oil painting that hangs over the couch and the two items are

116

linked in color by a dish of coordinated candy in a crystal bowl on the coffee table. Placed carefully throughout every room are the right bibelots that Randy has spent literally hundreds of hours ferreting out in smart shops. There is a menagerie in china and glass, ranging from an elephant end table to a crouching china cat, complete with glaring blue glass eyes and fake fuzz, which stares up from the floor at the tiny crystal mice at play on a shelf above. The collection is completed by a grinning porcelain monkey, whose arms are wrapped over its head, and whose eyes stare at the room in an expression of glazed madness.

One wag has since suggested that the porcelain chimp was actually modeled on the lady's husband. But if anyone thinks that Mr. Perfect Prince is unappreciative, they have a small surprise in store. He wants the glamorous, *au courant* surroundings as much as she does. In all of the homes I visited, not one Jewish Prince expressed a murmur of dismay over sleeping on pink and yellow pastel flowered sheets with ruffly pillow covers and matching lacy, eyelet quilt. The kitchen is the only area in which a prince's demands may stymie the princess' dreams. Since most Jewish boys are raised in homes where traditional plain eaters thrive on the boiled chicken-in-a-pot and kasha and pot roast circuit, they are not accustomed to caviar, capers or chicory. The Perfect Princess must toss out Julia Child for Jennie Grossinger. One princess who studied haute cuisine for six months spent an entire afternoon making her debut dish to be served at home. After three sweaty hours over the stove, she proudly served a Capon Wellington for dinner. Her husband prodded it with a knife, then looked up and asked, "What is that? A raisin challah?" So much for the status stomach.

Though she may not be a gourmet chef, the Perfect Princess sets a gorgeous table, a picture from *House and Garden*. Exquisite flowered china, delicate crystal goblets, tiny sterling silver ash trays, fresh flowers in cut glass vases, elaborate carved silver place settings, and stiff linen table cloth and lacy matching napkins. All of this was for lunch with a few friends. The menu was chef's salad tossed in a crystal bowl, croissants tucked into a sterling silver basket, bake shop cookies on a china plate and coffee from a huge silver pot. As the ladies filed in to luncheon, they could not get over how lovely everything looked. The warm rush of compliments began to flow over the hostess. "Oh, what a gorgeous table," "My, you really know how to do things right," "Everything looks so perfect, it's a shame to touch a thing." The hostess acknowledged the praise with a nod of her head. "It never fails that someone says how exquisite my tables are. Never." Inured to the compliments by now, she dismissed the admiration with a shrug. "My tables are always gorgeous," and the expression on her face indicated, so what else is new?

The luncheon hostess also took credit for the immaculate cleanliness of the manicured and polished house. Of course, she has "help" in every day, but those of us in the know are aware that even a maid requires the full-time participation of a Jewish Princess. After all, you must keep an eye out, you Never Know. When I called the lady about the lunch date, she told me, "I can't talk to you now, the cleaning girl is here." It made me stop and think for a moment.

118

The Perfect Princess

Keeping very, very busy is part of what the Perfect Princess is all about. She will tell you, "My husband and I lead such full lives we hardly ever see each other except at breakfast," and she will mean that to be an admirable accomplishment. She gets her hand into every single household task, from following the maid around and giving pillows an extra plump, to personally hand-picking every morsel of food in the refrigerator and cupboards. She is one lady who never, never orders by phone. "How could you? As my mother says, you never *know* what they'll give you!"

This Perfect Princess also involves herself with charities, Jewish organizations like "Federation" (Federation of Jewish Philanthropies) or secular groups such as the American Cancer Society. As a carry-over from her tasteful, organized life, she will often get involved in planning the dinner dance, on the decorating, food or entertainment committee. She is known for snaring chic raffle prizes and high-class entertainment because of her "connections." More serious community-affairs-oriented women regard the Perfect Princess as the lightweight, or "fluffy" member, but when it is time for the annual Spring Fashion Show, the group makes good use of her talents. Inevitably, she is asked to model some of the clothes. And that is being "constructive," as one princess puts it.

Obviously, the life of a Perfect Princess is as demanding and exhausting a profession as any outside job. Like the traditional Jewish wife of old, who ran the house, the store and the finances while her husband studied the Torah, the Perfect Princess is once again an administrator.

And though by definition, a working woman cannot be

119

an undiluted Perfect Princess (where would she ever get the time?), she may be surprised to learn she has the potential. Some career women cannot associate themselves with these girls; in fact, they have chosen to go to work full-time in order to avoid being a full-blown, stay-at-home Jewish Princess. But regardless of the working woman's distaste for the homebound, perfect world, lurking in the personality structure are elements of Barbara, reminding them to reupholster the chairs, plump the couch pillows and serve at least three kinds of hors d'oeuvres to any dinner guest.

And in addition, the drive, the busyness, and the dedication of the Perfect Princess are readily apparent in the striving for career success found in young Jewish women out in the professional world. Just as Barbara has worked endless hours to make certain her home life is perfect, so too will a Jewish Princess work hard and long to become an acknowledged success in her chosen field.

7

WILL SUCCESS SPOIL THE JEWISH PRINCESS?

> From that she makes a living?
> —Update of a familiar saying

A new kind of achievement is available to a Jewish Princess today, apart from simply marriage and family. She merely applies her inbred drive and self confidence to any particular career. With her nerve, kineahorah, and such confidence, a princess can do anything she chooses.

Of course, her family does not anticipate such career success. Momma and Poppa did not raise her to become chairman of the board. She is supposed to get married "That's the only career for her," the parents agree. "She should know better." Often they are hard pressed to understand why their daughter would want to work so hard. Or, how she can postpone the glorious moment of childbirth (or as the parents see it, the advent of grandchildren).

But they have also raised their daughter to believe in herself, and as a result, they may have a career woman on their hands, a Jewish Princess who utilizes the advantages of her cherished childhood in an effort to "make it" professionally.

121

The career-oriented princess possesses certain distinct advantages over her ambitious peers. She is able to work in an atmosphere relatively free from the fear of failure. She knows damn well she will not starve. (Whoever heard of a starving Jewish anything?) And if things do not go too well, there is always the emotional and economic support of the family to fall back on. But her secure background has not made the princess "soft." She is no pampered child, demanding "I want" without lifting a finger. When a Jewish Princess decides what she is after and sets out to get it, she can be as tough as any of the competition.

Though the young women I interviewed were raised in fairly well-to-do Jewish homes, they all have chosen the harder route to fame and fortune. Interestingly enough, they share one common advantage: each was raised as the only daughter in the family.

Despite the goyish name, Julia Miller Phillips is a Jewish Princess, and, at age thirty, a smashing success. She recently collected an Oscar as one of three producers of the Newman-Redford hit film *The Sting.* Like every Jewish girl, Julia loves to talk and even with eleven new Hollywood productions under way, she kept me entertained on the phone for more than an hour.

"What do you think about Jewish Princesses?" I began by asking her.

"Wait a second," said Julia. "I have an important call, can you hold on a minute?"

"Sure," I said.

"Okay, I'm putting you on hold."

I was promptly disconnected.

Julia called back, apologetic. "Sorry, really. I guess the hold button isn't working."

"So what about the Jewish Princess?" I began again, and Julia said, "Wait a minute. I've gotta get a cigarette. They're in the other room. Do you mind?"

"No," I said.

"It'll only take me a minute to get them," she said, then laughed out loud. "Well, you shouldn't mind. After all, it's my dime."

At long last, three thousand miles away, Julia settled in with a cigarette to chat over her bedroom phone as she looked at a stretch of Malibu beach and the Pacific Ocean outside her window. This time, I started in by asking her specifically about Oscar night, 1974, when she picked up her Academy Award.

"Michael, my husband, and I were dressed for the night by this guy who is aces in costume design. He said that everyone thought of me as a New York girl and they'd expect me to look a certain way. So he decided I'd wear black, not white or a flowery print like the California people. The dress was a Halston, and I had a boa around my neck, black and white feathers. I think it had some guinea feathers in their somewhere."

Julia said she couldn't run up right away to collect her award because she got stuck in her seat. "My pearls were caught in the chair," she recalled.

For the benefit of posterity (and correctness), she repeated her acceptance speech verbatim: "You can't imagine what a trip it is for a Jewish girl from Great Neck to win an Academy Award and meet Elizabeth Taylor on the same night!"

Needless to say, Great Neck was not the only spot which reacted to this amusing remark. In Hollywood, Julia said they misunderstood her completely. "I was really being ironical, using Great Neck metaphorically. I only lived there four years, but it seemed to say it all. That night, a lot of people rushed up and told me they thought it was a very 'human' thing to say. Only the really sharp people, like Walter Matthau and Jack Lemmon, understood that I was being funny."

"And what did your mother think?"

"She thought the award was great, I mean she was happy I'd won and all, but she also told me, 'Julia, I assume you won't wear those chicken feathers with that dress again!'"

Perhaps Julia was not as ironical as she believed, I thought to myself. Apparently you can take the Jewish Princess from Great Neck, but you can't take the suburban Jewish ghetto from the princess. And Halston dress, Oscar, Robert Redford and Hollywood aside, Julia is very "from." Haimisheh.

As Julia tells it, she was raised quite modestly when compared with the solid-gold standards of the grassy principality which is Great Neck, Long Island. "A Jewish Princess is what I wasn't," Julia insisted, and provided an instant back-up list of Why Nots. In the Miller household, freshly moved from Brooklyn, conspicuous consumption was toned down to a manageable level. The Millers drove a

Plymouth, joined a pool club (no fancy golf course or clubhouse, just the concrete and water) and initiated Julia into the world of books. Told to "Read!" by her literary parents, she listened obediently. "Of course, I didn't have to go off to the public library like other less fortunate people," Julia recalled. Then, listening to herself, quickly added, "Boy, do I sound snotty."

The Millers ignored many of the correct suburban puberty rites, but did attempt to send Julia to camp. Characteristically, Julia refused. From ages four to thirteen, Julia got carted off to the beach instead, because she suffered from what she described as "an allergy to my own sweat." Each year, even before the school term had ended, Julia and her younger brother were plucked from their classes the minute the temperature climbed a drop over seventy degrees and ferried out to Fire Island where they spent the entire hot summer.

She may not have driven in a Cadillac or golfed at a country club, but Julia received the requisite Jewish Princess education in the value of success. All through high school, Julia said, "My mother plagued me. She wanted me to achieve something of value, a major accomplishment, in writing. She thought I had a higher talent." Something like *War and Peace*? I asked. "Probably yes," Julia answered. "Something of significance is what my mother had in mind. And, since we were always the less wealthy family in a well-to-do area, my mother let me know it was also important to make money, a good deal of money."

Julia recalled her college years as highly unsuccessful. "I

barely got through," she said unflinchingly. There was a try at writing, an unpublished novel which seemed to indicate to Julia that writing books and earning money were not exactly compatible. And a few problems with the constraint of proper Mount Holyoke. "I wasn't any great rebel, but I never took too well to rules. Let's say I was a quiet rebel."

When Julia decided to marry Michael Phillips, a nice Jewish boy from Roslyn, Long Island, the year after her graduation in 1965, she rebelled a bit more openly. No big wedding, she insisted, after attending dozens of gala affairs given by her friends' families. She was wed at the St. Moritz (right on) but with a guest list of seventy (small by princess standards) and a judge (for a Jewish couple, the ultimate no-no). "It caused a great deal of strife, especially the judge," she recalled. But Julia knew what she wanted.

What our girl from Great Neck wanted most of all was a career. She was not sure what career, but in a bow to Momma she took a job writing for a salary, in magazine work. She started as a production assistant at *McCall's*. Eight months later, she went to the *Ladies' Home Journal*. Two years passed before another moment of truth confronted Julia. "They promoted me to associate editor but gave me a disgusting raise of only one thousand dollars a year. Can you believe that?" She decided to quit the field forever.

A friend from magazine days thought Julia oughta be in pictures, and offered her a spot as a story editor at Paramount. With a kind of "why not?" attitude and some interest in the glamour of the movie business, she accepted. "I worked eventually for several companies including Paramount, Mirisch, First Artists. I learned the ins and outs of finding material for specific directors. I was their East Coast representative. After I became friends with some Hollywood people, I guess Robert Redford was my first real show biz friend, I discovered most stars were cash poor. They didn't have the money to option properties they wanted for themselves since their money was tied up in investments, real estate or lavish life styles." From that observation, came Julia's idea, carried out by the Phillipses and Tony Bill, whom Julia met at First Artists: "A cash fund, venture capital, to help the artists option properties."

Together, the three decided their first investment would be two properties written by David S. Ward, *Steelyard Blues* and *The Sting*. And, incredibly enough, with all the dozens and dozens of writers and scripts floating around Hollywood, the Bill/Phillips Production team chose a real winner. Why the great success right away? Julia attributes it to luck. "That goes for us as much as anything else does. We're all interested in gambling."

Up until this first investment in Hollywood, Michael and Julia lived unpretentiously in Manhattan while Michael completed his law degree and worked on Wall Street. But with work in Hollywood about to go into full swing in 1971, the Phillipses moved West. And what a revelation that change was for the former Long Islanders. Obviously, neither Great Neck nor Roslyn could compare.

"We could not believe the way people lived out here!" Julia gasped, still overwhelmed even after spending three and a half years in Hollywood. "We didn't like Beverly Hills and Brentwood. You should see the way the houses are done. When we first started looking, we were amazed. People have sunken baths, sunken living rooms, sunken beds, sunken everything! Jacuzzi whirlpool baths. The real estate agents take you through these labyrinths of rooms and then they say, 'And here is the master bedroom *suite*.' It was too much."

The Phillipses settled into a beachside rental, in the "less fashionable" part of Malibu, Julia quickly pointed out. She lives in the same house today, but not with Michael. The two are amicably separated (only in Hollywood!), but Julia is still adjusting. Later, she referred to her marital woes as "my worst Karma." They have a ten-month-old daughter, Kate, and Julia has hired a pleasant, full-time housekeeper to watch her. "But I can't wait until Kate's older and more mobile," said Julia excitedly. "I want to try taking her into work with me."

Baby Kate will then accompany Julia on her fifty-mile drive to the Burbank Studios where Momma is immersed in the near-dozen new films the company has in the planning or shooting stage. With that long commute in mind, I asked Julia if she drives an expensive, fast, Hollywood-style car, maybe a Jaguar or Porche. But no, Julia putt-putts to work daily in a Mazda. "I was never very big on property," she explained. "I've never even gotten it together to assemble an entire house. I just don't feather my nest too well."

If Julia's fulfillment does not lie on a material level, apparently her drive to succeed in her work knows no

128

bounds. "My need to achieve is something much more than an Oscar can fulfill," she said very matter-of-factly. "All your life you're taught to believe certain things give you a rush. The Oscar didn't." What is necessary in Julia's career, to give her real satisfaction, is creative achievement. "Creativity" for Julia, she said, means working on projects she loves, hashing out themes with the writers, talking about the "vision" she sees in a property and seeing it through to production. Naturally, with the artistic end in mind, it should not be surprising to learn Julia wants to direct, as well.

And the great push toward a valuable achievement is a product of her background, Julia admitted. She calls her inner strivings "my demons," in a tongue-in-cheek fashion, and went on to describe an encounter with a good friend at a recent party to indicate how strongly her drive comes across. "He came up to me and said, 'You know, your demons are what's so repellent and seductive about you.'" Does Julia agree with the assessment? "Yes. My mother bedeviled me all my life, to use my higher intelligence, to make a contribution. Look at my brother, he's three years younger than I am. A Harvard *summa* and a PhD from Princeton. He's a scientist, in solid-state physics. But I know that what he really wants to do is work on something original that will win him a Nobel Prize."

Demons aside, Julia's mother also told her to earn money, and that she has done. Loads of money is pouring in. Where will it go? "Ask me in two weeks, when I get my biggest *Sting* check so far," she said. "I'll probably buy my own house now, on the beach, and fix it up. Lately I've been getting the urge to paint and decorate. And I know I'll blow quite a few thousand on clothes I've wanted to own. I used to be a clothes horse, before I got pregnant. Now, since Kate, I have hips." Julia would obviously love to spend some of her loot back in New York, where East Coast style still has its lure for the former Long Island princess. When I asked Julia what she missed most about New York, she did not say her parents or her friends. She said, with no hesitation, "Bendel's. Whenever I go to New York, I hop across to Bendel's and drop a fortune on shoes." Anything else? "Yes, I miss my hairdresser, Victor, at Pierre Michel. He cuts my hair the best. Out here, they just try to follow the lines. Like all Jewish girls, I'm a hair freak. I wash it every day. I can't bear dirty hair."

Suddenly, Julia's voice changed from finicky princess to crooning Jewish momma, as she said, "Hello, hello Kate," to the baby who crawled into her room. It prompted me to ask, "Will your daughter be a Jewish Princess?"

Julia laughed, and replied, "With a name like Kate Phillips?" Then she added, "If you're pretty, which I was, your parents treat you as a princess. I see this same feeling in how I am with Kate. She gets away with things by being adorable and manipulative, and that's princesslike."

But despite all of the success and fame which have come Julia's way, the overall impression of the Hollywood producer was, for me, a sense of a little girl in front of the candy store window. Julia is wistful, somehow believing she has not really achieved any great success at all. She waits to make the great contribution her family always expected of her. And that apparently is more than the Hollywood equivalent of the Nobel Prize.

On the other hand, there are Jewish Princesses who find career success does satisfy their intense desire to achieve. Broadway producer Maxine Fox, a nice Jewish girl from Baltimore, is on top with such shows as *Grease* and *Over Here.* Though she is eager for more hits in the future, her present achievements have made her glow with satisfaction. At twenty-nine, Maxine finds she is quite fulfilled.

I headed up to meet Maxine at the offices of Fox and Waissman Productions. Waissman is Maxine's husband, Ken, another nice Jewish kid from Baltimore. The two work in the grungy, backstage atmosphere provided by the old Palace Theater building. A theaterwise elevator man took me up to their floor, while gossiping nonstop with a script-toting passenger of great, handsome, actorish good looks. Inside the producers' offices, I waited for Maxine, staring at the trophies of theatrical success displayed on one outer office wall, the cardboard posters from their shows. First, *Fortune and Men's Eyes,* done off-Broadway in 1969, then Julie Harris' Broadway vehicle *And Miss Reardon Drinks a Little,* 1971, followed by their two current musical hits. Not bad for five years' work, I thought as I waited.

A young woman approached me, whom I immediately pegged as a secretary. She extended a hand, and said warmly, "Hi! I'm Maxine Fox," in a lowish, sultry voice that did not fit her appearance. She looks rather like a high school cheerleader, short, compact, athletically built, and peppy. Her tan is set off by golf clubby clothes, white slacks, sleeveless, printed orange and blue nylon top, white sandals. She has big, dark eyes, and wears lightly tinted aviator-style glasses. Her dark hair is cut Dutch boy fashion, with bangs curving down to her eyebrows. Her smile is wide and friendly. But the impression is suburban, relaxed, and casual instead of Manhattan chic and elegant. This is the lady producer?

"Want to meet Ken?" she asked. I nodded, and we walked into their shared office, a spacious, sunny corner room with nondistinct decor featuring two wooden desks and an upright piano. Framed newspaper clippings look at least five years old, as though no one cares to keep up with the barrage of newer stories. Ken was on the phone. He looked up and said "Hello," with a wholesome smile. I felt as though I was back in high school and had just met the two kids unanimously voted Most School Spirit. At Maxine's suggestion, we retired to a back office to talk.

I noticed that Maxine has no diamond, just a twisted gold wedding band. But she is loaded with the old competitive spirit. The only daughter and special first child of working parents (partners in advertising), Maxine grew up in a family in which achievement was taken for granted. Even at age six, when she took her first ballet lessons and fell in love with the stage, Maxine never doubted that she would be anything but a stunning success.

Like Julia Phillips, Maxine was raised in a fairly well-off, middle-class Jewish environment. Was she pampered? No, she said, because pampered means the parents indulge themselves. Spoiled? Yes, because spoiling means a show of love. There was "the obligatory temple Sunday School bit," confirmation, ballet, jazz and modern dance lessons, a cabana at Atlantic City, New Jersey, for the summer, orthodontia, camp, and piano lessons, until the day Maxine refused to cut her fingernails to practice. That was the end of the piano. But beyond all of the little niceties, the Foxes gave their daughter some helpful advice. "There's no formula for success," they told her. "Whatever you want is possible. The impossible? Just takes a little longer." Maxine said, "My parents taught me that the one common denominator of success was knowing you're going to be successful. In my special case, it was my awareness of New York City and my love of the theater. If I wanted to be the best, I had to be with the best."

"The best" in theater meant Broadway, and so eighteen-year-old Maxine left Boston University after one year and headed for Times Square. Quit is not a word she uses, because she left college with every intention of returning one day.

Maxine's college education continued behind the footlights, and backstage, as she worked her way from summer, "tent" theater (so-called because shows are staged under a tent), to the Big Time. Broadway. Maxine's first major show was *Funny Girl,* a stint as production assistant, following which she worked for six months as Barbra Streisand's personal secretary ("that was all I could take"), and then back to shows. Production work on *Sweet Charity, Mame, You're A Good Man, Charlie Brown,* and then the big step out on her own, taken with coworker and boyfriend Ken Waissman.

While the two worked together, they also lived together, making their parents more than just a little edgy. Both sets of proper Baltimorians were dying for their kids to get married, but Ken and Maxine resisted several years of what Maxine called rather whimsically, "the wind on our backs," until a spur-of-the-moment impulse in, of all places, Las Vegas.

As Maxine tells it, these two typical Jewish kids were walking down the bustling streets of neon-lit, smarmy Vegas in the middle of the night, when the 24-hour-a-day chapels caught their eyes. Why not? They decided. First, a license was secured at the all-night license bureau, and then the couple took a walk down the main drag in search of the proper setting. The two Jewish easterners in Vegas had only one requirement for their wedding chapel: it should not have a large display featuring a huge cross. Their chapel had to be, if not Jewish, at least not Christian. Maxine and Ken finally settled on the services of a judge at a nonsectarian wedding parlor, a choice made on the basis of true high class clout. "We picked a chapel that took American Express instead of one which accepted Master Charge. When you go big, you really have to go all the way," said Maxine. And so the Waissmans were wed, charging it to Maxine's credit card. After the ceremony, they called their parents, even though the hour was very late back in Baltimore. And as final proof that to Jewish parents, married is married regardless of where it happens, the Foxes and Waissmans were overjoyed. And relieved.

But Maxine added quickly, "Our parents better not wait for grandchildren."

"No Pampers on the horizon?" I asked. "What do your folks think?"

"There really isn't that much of a pull on us to have kids. Our parents know it's possible," Maxine said. Well, I thought, give them time. Las Vegas was only a year ago.

As Maxine and Ken rake in the loot from their Broadway successes, they plow most of it back into new projects. Maxine's ideas of how to spend her personal money are not very unusual. She wants clothes that are "good, and made well," and said this leads some people to believe she is a real clothes horse. She assured me she is not. Maxine would also love an occasional game of tennis. Ken, a sedentary Jewish Prince, does not play. Though the couple lives in a duplex apartment, Maxine's chatter does not include one detail of furnishing or decorating. All of that seems to bore her. Naturally, she prefers talk about Broadway.

"I'm very lucky to have the success now," said Maxine, "but if I don't keep going, looking for new challenges, it doesn't stay. I put so much of my love and life and emotion into my work. We have to fall in love with any property we do. And I'm always striving for the best."

The particular attraction of the theater, for Maxine, she summed up as "the very special thing that happens sitting in a theater. I was drawn to it because it was so special."

As we got up to leave, Maxine added, "I'm an achiever at things I'm vitally interested in. For Jewish women, there's always this feeling of drive, even for a girl who counts the size of her diamond or her number of minks as important."

Minkless and diamondless Maxine Fox shares a common notion with Julia Phillips: Both reject outright the preconceived idea that they are "typical JPs." They deemphasize any of the material, marital and maternal chozzerai that means "Princess" to them.

But one has to ask about the Jewish Princess who comes from the truly cushy, luxurious background. Is she going to have the same drive as a middle-class girl, to "make it" big in a career? Some answers to my questions are provided by Dena Kaye. The Beverly Hills child of show business royalty, Danny Kaye and Sylvia Fine, Dena chose not to stay in California and not to work in the entertainment field. Declining the role of a Candice Bergen or a Heather MacRae, Dena wanted to be successful on her own, in a different part of the country and in her own chosen field, journalism.

But success does not come easily to struggling writers in New York and Dena is no exception. She has a nice title, assistant editor, at the *Saturday Review/World* magazine, but the truth is that she answers someone else's phone. Though she does publish pieces under her own by-line and has done a good deal of traveling while researching her articles, she must find spare time after work, frequently, to polish her stories. She is not as high-powered or successful as Julia Phillips or Maxine Fox. But that does not mean she would not like to be. After all, Dena too is a Jewish Princess.

She lives in an apartment she proudly informs me she decorated herself, a cheerful, lush, tropical paradise with an atmosphere of Hollywood on the Hudson, Casablanca à la California. White wicker furniture, bright orange and yellow print cushions, flowers floating in bowls of water and yards of bright, plush, grass green carpet. The place is neat, clean and shining.

And Dena, too, is scrubbed-looking. Very much the princess in dress (a blue pants outfit, blue suede sandals to match, streaky blond hair, makeup and the proper gold jewelry), she has more of a healthy, outdoors California look than a lot of the skinnier, whiter, East Coast princesses with whom I am most familiar. Her eyes are blue. I guess they grow them differently in Beverly Hills.

A pleasant, homey hostess, Dena asks me what I would like to drink, and although I only ask for water, she brings me a huge tumbler full, loaded with ice cubes. We gossip about mutual friends in the publishing world before we begin the "official questions."

"Were you the special, favored child in the family?" I asked.

Her blue eyes grew very large. "Of course. I was an only child, and Danny Kaye's daughter." As she began to describe her life, I decided that being spoiled for Dena is a lot different than it is for you and me.

First, there was home, Beverly Hills, no less. Suburban Jewish paradise sublime, what with swimming pools, chauffered cars, super-expensive homes, and all of those posh, chichi boutiques. Dena's first school was progressive, private, multiracial and aggressively casual. Blue jeans, camping trips and dramatic presentations replaced home-work and grades. After this liberated elementary education, the grade-grubbing at Beverly Hills High School was somewhat startling for Dena. "I was great at languages, but I did have a couple of math tutors," she recalled. High school was also where those California kids showed off their newest acquisitions, especially cars. A car is the sign of status in a freeway society. By age sixteen, Dena decided it was her turn, too. She asked Mom and Dad for a car. "No," they said. "Please?" asked Dena. "We don't want to spoil you," said the Kayes. "Spoil me?" Dena answered. "It's ridiculous. Everywhere I go I have to get driven by the butler and you don't want me to be spoiled?" She got the car.

But the course of life for a Hollywood princess does not always run so smooth. There was the time when young Dena enrolled in ballet classes and came home one day to inform her puzzled mother, "I quit." When Mrs. Kaye asked why, her daughter informed her, "Daddy didn't take dancing lessons to learn how to dance." Patiently, Dena's mother sat her child down and explained to her that Danny Kaye spent a good many years touring with a troupe, working out the problems in his act. Dena recalled, "I didn't understand that, then." What she wanted was to be instantly talented, as her parents seemed to be. She did not continue dancing classes. And when the traditional question of music lessons arose, Dena said, "I took up guitar because my mother was a pianist."

Despite much of the pampering of a Beverly Hills adolescence, Dena pointed out she did not travel abroad until she was sixteen. "I did fly to summer camp in the East (the East Coast), but camp was still camp. My parents traveled all over because of the Business, but I did not grow up oriented to the world."

Perhaps that sense of being homebound for so long has

contributed to Dena's main ambition at the present time: to do more extensive work on travel articles, to go to places that she finds exciting and work on a book. Admittedly, she has a long, long way to go to fulfill those dreams but she insists they are within the realm of possibility. "My writing? I don't consider it just something to do. I see writing as a lifelong interest," she said.

Working hard and long hours after a full day's work at the magazine, Dena has written pieces which have appeared in *Cosmopolitan,* the Los Angeles *Times* and *New York* magazine, as well as the *Saturday Review/World.* But she seems restless and not at all content with her assistant editorship. I wonder, then, if at twenty-seven Dena would be interested in settling for the more common Jewish Princess path to success: marriage.

Her answer? At the moment, no. "Being single, living alone, is important for me, to find out what I need."

"Do your parents press you about marriage?" I asked.

"No," she said.

And Danny Kaye, famous for publicly kissing, loving and entertaining thousands of international small fry for UNICEF does not nudge his only daughter about grandchildren. As Dena coolly said, "Motherhood is a private thing, something I've got to work out."

Dena and I wind up our conversation with Dena asking me if I wanted to hear about a friend of hers, this "real Jewish Princess." "Go ahead," I told her.

"She's a great girl, and she has absolutely everything," Dena said. "A rich husband, two in help, an apartment overlooking the park, two gorgeous children."

As Dena talked, I listened for a trace of envy in her voice. After all, this girlfriend of hers has everything a princess like Dena was born to desire. And there have been no references to the lure of the Jewish Princess dream life in any of Dena's chatter about work and living alone. Apparently, that exquisite "good life" does not appeal.

"You take what you want from your background," Dena said. If not the luxurious trimmings, then what has Dena selected? "A subtle pressure to do well, to be the best. I'd like to be recognized as being particularly good for whatever kind of writing I'm doing," she answered.

And there was another legacy for Dena, from the Kaye household, something she mentioned just at the end of our interview. Dena was a beloved child. "Yes, I was adored, loved. There was always an exuberance in my family, a lot of physical love, hugging and kissing. You have a lot to give then, growing up that way, instead of being concerned with take, take, take."

Dena has been given the gift of the Jewish parent, the investment of love and attention which yields the personal dividend of confidence. Not every Jewish Princess is totally self-confident one hundred percent of the time, but generally, if she is working toward some particular goal, I challenge anyone to tell her she will never make it. Behind Dena's talk of achieving something of value in the writing world is that familiar intensity, that drive to succeed possessed by Julia Phillips and Maxine Fox. But Dena proves that even the comparatively less successful Jewish Princess remains undeterred. And would a Broadway flop or a box office bomb faze Ms. Fox or Ms. Phillips? I doubt it.

Julia, Maxine and Dena each express an unfulfilled, wistful quality about work, a sense of "Have I really done enough? Am I that successful?" coupled with disbelief, "Can this really happen to a nice Jewish girl from a gilded ghetto?" Obviously, yes, it can. Being raised as a special child often results in a strong drive to be special in a particular field.

And where that drive is directed leads us to consideration of the next question. What about the Jewish woman's choice of career? No one should be surprised to discover that she has no qualms about rising to the challenge of the most difficult, time-consuming, exhausting professions. And, in the process, becoming famous enough to have her name become that oft-cited, familiar "household word." On all levels of occupation, the Jewish Princess has arrived. Mazeltov!

8

MY DAUGHTER, THE DOCTOR

"I couldn't be a real Jewish Princess," said a young surgical resident in a crumpled white jacket and skirt. "After all, I have to deal with vomit."

People playing a game of group therapy would probably not free associate "princess" with blood pressure, urine specimens or paramecium. But young Jewish women *are* working in surgery, pediatrics, internal medicine and obstetrics. They are also becoming lawyers, architects, politicians and even stewardesses. Granted there may be no "Fly Naomis" in the TV ads and the most current Dr. Cohens in the phone books are male. But at this moment, a new wave of Jewish women is ready to take on the challenge of all available professions.

Jewish Princess cool can amaze skeptical male professional peers. Interns at one of the country's top medical centers reported on a scene which occurred regularly on their morning rounds. As a group of new doctors was led around the wards by an attending physician, they were asked questions and opinions regarding various cases.

143

With the exception of two young women, the group was male. All the interns were fresh from four years at various prestigious medical schools. The women were both Jewish, and were described in a slightly shocked but grudgingly respectful way by one of the male doctors as "incredible. We went from bed to bed, and each time a question was asked or they were called on to speak, they answered with total confidence. Their answers were phrased as though they were absolutely certain they had the correct reply. The rest of us stood around quaking in our shoes. And there were quite a few guys from Harvard and Yale Med in that group. But no one had the nerve these girls showed." Pass the bedpan, Harry.

A lawyer in San Francisco gave a similar report on several of his female, Jewish colleagues. He was quick to note that they had made an impression not only on his firm, but also on other members of the California bar. In his immortal words, "The women have what I'd call Jewish Princess balls. When I deal with them, on cases or in the courtroom, I can see that they may be Jewish Princesses. But they use that quality professionally and make it work." How does one use princessness on the job? Easy, the lawyer said. "They're used to having their own way and they never entertain the thought of failure. With that attitude, they know they'll get ahead."

For instance, one young graduate of Harvard Law School took a job with a prestigious Wall Street firm. She was one of a select number of the crème de la crème admitted to the office each year. After twelve months, she was looking for another job. Why? "I couldn't take being just one of the dozens of young, brilliant lawyers they had hand-selected. Everyone was slaving hard for recognition, but we all knew we wouldn't get as far as we wanted to go within the next few years. There were just too many brilliant people doing the same thing. Everyone was trying for one of the few openings higher up." Was she afraid she wouldn't get one of those slots? "No, I probably would," she said matter-of-factly. "But I decided to join a smaller firm instead, where my abilities would be recognized faster." A mensh.

But there was always a handful of Jewish women who made it from poor to powerful, who have not had what we defined in this book as typical princess upbringings, but nevertheless became the first Jewish-American professional women. Mollie Parnis, one of the best known American couturieres, began in the garment industry. While working, it soon became apparent to her that she had to make it or spend the rest of her life doing piecework at a sewing machine.

Our interview took place far away from the scene of her childhood in the 1900's as the daughter of Austrian immigrants. We met in the cool, brightly-lit beige showroom that is Parnis-Livingston, Inc. Mollie Parnis is chic, vibrant, and in modern lingo, super-together. There is something motherly about her, but when you watch her in action the tough, business side comes out. She knows from the struggle to survive.

As I entered the showroom, Mollie, a white-blond woman in a black dress, greeted me, "Hello, I'm Mollie Parnis. Would you mind waiting a moment while I talk to some people?" I sat down on a beige Louis-the-something chair as she attended to her work. She looks rather unprepossessing, in her black frock, with her hair styled in a short, crisp style brushed away from her face. She wears simple jewelry, gold chains, a watch, a chunky gold charm around her neck. She stares you straight in the eye, her handshake is firm, and she gives you a sharp, alert glance that is an instant, on-the-spot sizing up. Certainly, she appears to be in her sixties, an unfacelifted, fairly natural woman. But she shows her smarts openly, no attempt to be girlish, youthful or falsely humble. She is clearly The Boss.

She does not look glamorous, but what occurs all around her in her fashion business is. The Seventh Avenue showroom scene is stagey, exciting and dramatic to see. As I waited for Miss Parnis to finish talking to some buyers, I watched her models walk through the carpeted showroom to the boutique next door, where they showed evening wear to several clients. The models who wear the clothes are frisky and teasing before entering the boutique, then they glide in with self-possessed cool. Opposite the boutique, on the other side of the showroom, are a changing room, offices and work space, into which people pass with regularity, fitters with tape measures, bent ladies in space shoes with eyeglasses on a chain around their necks, and sharp young men in platform-soled shoes whose presence does not bother the models in their underwear.

My attention was drawn back to Mollie Parnis as she and her buyers finished their work, choosing fashions for a charity show in Texas. Her timing was perfect, I noticed.

She said very little but when she spoke, she chose to do so carefully, with firmness, saving her words for moments when a final decision was necessary. Then what she had to say was crisp, precise, to the point. When she was through with the buyers, she showed them to the door, chatted with them for a few polite moments, and then turned to me.

"Now we can begin," she said, motioning to me to follow her. We walked into her office, a large room opposite the models' changing area. As we talked, Mollie left her door open, and could watch what was going on in the models' changing room across the hall.

Her own office is carpeted, with a handsome, carved wooden desk, shelves behind and a couch on the opposite wall. Though curtained, wide and air-conditioned, there is nothing frilly or lavish about the place. The space looks used, cluttered with piles of books and Mollie's special possessions, like the large, autographed color photo of Lyndon Johnson which sits, framed, on a shelf behind her.

Everyone outside her private life knows her as Mollie Parnis, but those who work for her in her home call her Mrs. Livingston. She is mother of a son, Robert, now a forty-year-old theatrical producer. As Mollie Parnis, she started with nothing and built up one of the most successful fashion empires in the country.

An immigrant's daughter, she was born in 1905 (according to *Current Biography*) or 1910 (so said the lady herself), the oldest of five children. "I know now we were poor," Mollie said. "My mother worked very hard. My father died when I was twelve. But at the time, I didn't realize how poor we were. Everyone around me was in the same situation, no one was very different. The Jews, the Italians, the Irish. We got our new pair of shoes every year at Passover, they got theirs at the same time, for Easter. When I was about fourteen, I began to realize there was a better world outside. It was then I became truly aware that if I ever did make it, there were certain things I could have. For example, I didn't realize till then that some people had two houses. But my family had lots of love and affection and I don't remember suffering."

But after her father's death when Mollie was twelve, doing well took on another side. "My mother had a terrible time just surviving. One of the things that goes back to that time was that I always had to survive. Those of us who could, did so by being creative, by doing what came naturally. But more and more the word survival comes back to me, behind everything I have done." She nodded her head, satisfied she had hit on exactly the right word. She repeated it throughout our talk.

What Mollie's mother had in mind for her eldest daughter was fairly typical: some job, and, of course, marriage. "My mother thought her sons and her daughters would do something professional, the sons doctors or lawyers, the daughters teachers. I broke my mother's heart when I said I wouldn't be a teacher. So I told her I'd be a lawyer instead. When I finally decided to be a designer, she thought I was crazy."

"When did you get interested in the whole Seventh Avenue scene?" I asked.

"I got a job when I was a junior at Hunter College, to work in a showroom for the summer. I liked it so much I never went back to college," Mollie recalled.

Did the family have a fit about that decision? "Nobody in my family was devastated when I wasn't going back to school. Although whenever possible I was spared the hardships, it was important to bring in money. The whole thing with Jews in America, even for Our Crowd, is a matter of survival."

The marriage push from Momma continued after Mollie went to work full time. Mrs. Parnis apparently believed that working as an assistant saleswoman in the showroom of a blouse manufacturer was no way to get a husband. And Mollie, single until her mid-twenties, gave her mother several years of aggravation. "I'm sure she was positive I'd be an old maid," Mollie said. "She never thought about my being successful in business."

After Mollie married textile specialist Leon Livingston, she left work for a few years. But when the two decided to set up their own firm in 1933, she returned to the fashion world for good. "I knew early on I was doing all right," she said firmly. "I never squandered time. Never worked more than nine to five. I hired other people, good people, and let them make decisions. And one of the first things I did, when I could, was get away from work at the end of the day, and not have people around me from the industry."

"Was it difficult being a part-time Jewish mother?" I asked her.

She nodded, and recalled how most wealthy women of the time had nurses and governesses. Then she noted proudly, "I always felt I spent more time with my child than the average mother. I always had a guilty feeling leaving him with a stranger. There is such a thing as a Jewish mother, a mother who cares, who wants education for her children, who wants more for them. But I do think my generation smothered our children, because we intended to spare them unpleasantness."

But times were still tough for a Jewish working momma. When Mollie applied to a posh boarding school for her son, she said she received quite a chilly letter in response. The reply said something to the effect of, "We don't want to accept the Livingston boy, we did not anticipate taking on any more Hebrew children," but went on to say they would allow him in. Her son received his private education entirely ignorant of the circumstances of his admission. His mother shielded him, just as she protected him from the financial hardships of her childhood by working hard in her business.

"I don't think my son would understand my kind of upbringing," she reflected. "I had to survive. But he was the son of fairly affluent parents, went to the best schools, private schools, Yale and Oxford. That's a natural Jewish trait, whatever you didn't have, you wanted for your children."

Success has also brought Mollie more than merely comfort and security for her family. She has the chance to meet and mingle with people she finds exceedingly interesting. "Oh, I'm gregarious," she said with a smile and a wave of her hand. "I like people and hope they like me. It's been a tremendous help in this business. I've worked with four President's wives, Eisenhower, Kennedy, Johnson and Nixon. And I've known two of the Presidents well, Eisenhower and Johnson. I've dined at the White House, they dined at my own home. I told them, 'Call me Mollie.' "

Mollie Parnis also entertains friends from other fields, whom she finds equally fascinating: journalists, theater people, writers. "I'm not the least bit interested in successful businessmen," the successful businesswoman said adamantly. "If one happens to be seated next to me at a dinner party, I don't want to hear about how he made all of his money."

Mollie Parnis is in many ways far from being today's standard "Jewish Princess," but she does serve as an example of exactly where more recent generations of Jewish women got their strength and push, part of the ethnic inheritance of Jewish women. The Mollies of the past were active, generous, busy, constructive women who worked uphill, against the odds, all their lives. Then what did Mollie Parnis think of today's so-called Jewish Princess?

"My generation had very few princesses," she pointed out. "And today, with so much going on in the world, how can you be more involved with yourself?"

I sensed her gorge rising on the subject, so I pressed her a bit further. "Do you think Jewish women today could go through what you have, to struggle to survive?"

The lady was firm, unequivocal. "No. I don't think so. I'll tell you a story that shows what I mean, from a trip I made to Israel a while ago. I was in Tel Aviv, talking with Mrs. Ben Gurion. I mentioned how nice it was to see all of the beautiful, new hotels that had been constructed there. And she turned to me, and said, 'We're not ready for them yet. The next generation will be too soft.'"

For Mollie Parnis, survival does not represent merely

living in a better neighborhood, having extra pairs of shoes and food on the table. Survival means success, and she doubts whether the more pampered modern generation can ever achieve the kind of hard-won success she did in her lifetime.

"You think the later generations do not have what it takes to make it in America?"

"Not the way we did," she replied. Then she phoned up her chauffeur, asked him to send the car around in thirty minutes, and showed me to the door.

I asked her a final question: "Was your need to 'survive' the push behind your success?"

She gave me one of her penetrating looks and said, "Yes. I took advantage of what was available at the time, which happened to be the garment business. In having to survive, I did what I could. If I hadn't survived, I'd be like one of the girls in the back."

But the girls in Mollie's back workroom have "survived," too. Then what is the difference between the way they survived and the way Mollie Parnis has survived? Simple. Ms. Parnis needed to rise to the top, and like many of her contemporaries, was not about to settle for any base level of subsistence, either for herself or for her family.

The legacy of wanting more has been carried through to the present, in the person of those Jewish women who feel that there is nothing too challenging or too impossible for their abilities. And Mollie Parnis is not entirely correct in her remark about the softness of today's generation. A look at their achievements in a wide variety of careers indicates that softness is a matter of attitude rather than affluence. If a woman wants to make a contribution of her own, financial security does not stand in the way. Jewish women in particular feel they have the strength to select the heretofore unconquered area and plunge right in. Their desire to succeed and not settle, is as sharp and as strong as the need in the past to feed a hungry family.

One young woman who has not shied away from making an impact of her own is a levelheaded lady from Flatbush, a politician, Congresswoman Elizabeth Holtzman, a Democrat from Brooklyn's sixteenth Congressional District.

Though in the past many Congressional Representatives have been faceless, it is difficult to forget the men and women who participated in the historic impeachment proceedings conducted by the House Judiciary Committee. And, in particular, Elizabeth Holtzman, a startlingly young woman. What the cameras caught of her was not exactly the picture of a Jewish Princess. The viewer saw a woman certainly not much older than thirty, with eyeglasses, dark brown hair curled at ear length, and a serious expression on her face. Her manner in addressing the committee was low-keyed and very intense. She spoke in a firm, clear, but somewhat soft voice. I caught her occasionally sneaking a puff on a cigarette, but for the most part she sat with her hands demurely folded, examining notes and papers and listening carefully to the debate. At recess, when she stood, she seemed small, slender, perhaps just over five feet tall. Her clothes? Rather matronly, running to printed dresses with matching jackets.

But Representative Elizabeth Holtzman seems not to care much about clothes, hair, makeup, chic, or Jewish Princesses. She is directed, beamed in, and focused on her responsibilities to her constituents, her peer group, her political beliefs, and her sense of honor.

In talking with her, the overwhelming impression is first, how strong a commitment she has to accomplish what she has set out to do—to contribute something of value to the political system. And second, how her goals make her oblivious to things around her not related to her work.

A good part of her intense focus on her work comes from her childhood, growing up in a close-knit and intellectually keen middle-class Brooklyn family. The life of an unprincessy Jewish Princess began in the home atmosphere of serious talk generated by the father (a lawyer) and mother (a Russian professor, now chairman of the department at Hunter College), and always including the fraternal twins, Elizabeth and Robert. The son (and half-hour elder of the two) is now a New York neurosurgeon.

"Was there much difference in expectation for your brother?" I asked her.

None at all, the Congresswoman noted. "We were treated differently because we were two different people. My parents felt strongly that a woman, just because she's a woman, shouldn't ignore her talents or her interest in any professional field."

Like many other achievement-oriented Jewish Princesses, Elizabeth Holtzman benefited from her family's early encouragement and support. "My parents had tremendous confidence in both my brother and me, a respect for us both. They encouraged us to think well of ourselves, to explore our talents and use them. And they treated us as adults. I think that was very important."

No matter that Elizabeth Holtzman was raised seemingly oblivious of much of the material side of Jewish Princesshood. She is proof that a princess is not defined by the parallels of Pappagallos and perfectly matched sweater sets. She apparently learned that achieving is doing, and whatever you do, you do it well, lessons that no Jewish Princess ever forgets.

Electoral success and a herald of the future came at Abraham Lincoln High School when Robert and Elizabeth Holtzman were elected president and vice-president of the GO (student council) on a platform featuring such slogans as "Win with the Twins." The memory draws a laugh from the Congresswoman and a denial that the moment was the germ of her political career.

"I didn't think of politics then" she said. "I definitely anticipated I'd go to college, and I probably thought I'd go on to work for some graduate degree, but I didn't know what field."

College was Radcliffe, where she graduated *magna cum laude* in 1962. She majored in American literature and American history but chose law school over graduate school. "I had decided I didn't want to spend my life in academia," she recalled. "I felt law was a good way of using my talents in a nonacademic approach. I still didn't think of politics." After law school, there was a job with a Manhattan law firm. But it was only "by accident" that Ms.

155

Holtzman said she got her first taste of politics and the political life, when the Lindsay administration hired her in 1967 as an assistant to the mayor.

While overseeing duties in the parks, recreation and cultural affairs area, Elizabeth Holtzman felt the calling. Politics. What did the job provide for her that proved to be so different?

"I was fascinated by the work," she said. "It was very challenging, very interesting. I saw the commitment and concern with urban problems rising. First, there was a tremendous amount to be done and few dedicated, honorable people in government. Having seen what I'd seen there, I thought, 'I could do as good a job.' Then second, bureaucracy and red tape had been until then a cliché for me. When I saw them in operation, I had to try to fight them."

For the next few years, after work with the mayor, a job with the prestigious firm of Paul Weiss, Rifkind, Wharton and Garrison, and election to the post of Democratic State Committeewoman in Flatbush, the goal of political office began to take shape. The opportunity to run arose in 1972, to challenge a forty-nine-year veteran of the House, Emanuel Celler, in the primary.

The fight for that seat was tough, as the press reported at the time, due to Celler's long incumbency and accrued power. But the lady who defeated him in a stunning upset will not look upon herself as a great dragon slayer or upset politician. Cool as ever, she noted that her victory was actually part of her advance planning. And if that is not true sangfroid, I don't know what is.

"The big decision for me was not to take Celler on, but

whether to run for Congress at all, whether I wanted to spend this kind of time in the business of politics. I thought very carefully about my decision," she recalled. "I was convinced I had an excellent chance of winning the election. What I finally did when I chose to run was based on two things. One, the sense that I'd win, and two, the enormous opportunity it presented to play some positive role in government policies."

That unrelenting confidence that would lead Elizabeth Holtzman to run in a race the newspapers and commentators believed next to impossible to win, that calm belief in herself, is the key to the woman. She gives the impression that it would take a great deal more than a difficult challenge to put her off the track; she stays cool and displays a toughness she herself fails to recognize.

"Are you tough?" I asked her.

"Tough?" She disliked the word immediately. "What do you mean? I'm not a violent person, I don't respect violence. I mean, ask my staff." She did not like any of the machismo implications of the word. "I really don't know about being tough."

But maybe something of the traditionally strong Jewish woman is behind Representative Holtzman's calm, directed demeanor. Even when she is under fire she stays incredibly steady. During the judiciary hearings, she was interrupted by Representative Charles Sandman of New Jersey, a moment which elicited a comment from Chairman Peter Rodino. "I think the gentlelady from New York can speak for herself," he said.

Representative Rodino knows his committee well. Ms. Holtzman did respond, swiftly and surely, to Mr.

Sandman. She laughed when I asked her about that moment, apparently enjoying the memory. Mr. Rodino's reply, she said, "pleased me. He expressed by his words that he felt I could handle myself and he said what he did out of experience, from what he knew. And then, I did respond to Mr. Sandman."

One of Elizabeth Holtzman's friends once told a newspaper reporter that Ms. Holtzman is "a very intense person who knows what she wants and knows how to get it." Since that remark completely suits the Jewish Princess, I asked Representative Holtzman (who says she does not know anything about princesses) if she identified with the comment.

Her response was, interestingly enough, affirmative. "I know often what I'd like to get. I think that's a very complimentary statement." Then she paused, and added modestly, "Of course, I'm still learning, finding out about the political system and how to operate in it."

She is no hotshot politico princess. Elizabeth Holtzman has all the princess' strengths but lacks a certain confidence in her self-assessments. It is nearly impossible to get her to compliment herself. Mention the word success and she counters with a little laugh. "A lot of people I know, friends and acquaintances, are not sure that being a Congresswoman is such a big cheese." How about the respect of colleagues in Congress? Was that hard for a Jewish woman to get, in a gentile, male-oriented institution? "No, if you do your homework, know what you talk about, and make sensible proposals, people listen to you," she commented.

Apparently, the Congresswoman works hard to ensure her position in the Congress. Her staff cites long days, stretching into the late evening and schedules jammed with an overflow of appointments and interviews. Has all of this gone to her head? Not at all. Congresswoman Holtzman prefers to underplay her role as any kind of big-time politician. Her Washington and Brooklyn staffs both comment on how hard she drives herself, the chairman of her House committee praises her on national TV, her parents worry about her health. But the strongest impression she gives is that she is doing exactly what she wants to do, driving herself hard because she knows no other way to accomplish the multitude of goals she has personally set for herself.

And back in Flatbush, her Jewish parents are, quite naturally, proud. "My parents think that, except for me, politics is a dirty business. But at this point, they understand the need for good people in government who do a lot of hard work and principled action." A daughter in politics still brings a good amount of naches to her mother. One member of Representative Holtzman's staff told me that on a drive to the Washington airport, a cab driver remarked to Mrs. Holtzman how lucky she was to be from Flatbush because of that great Congresswoman, Elizabeth Holtzman. "Do you know who that is?" Mrs. Holtzman said. "That's my daughter."

In Ms. Holtzman's career, and in the work of many other young Jewish women in different fields, there is ample proof that the present generation is no softer than any which preceded it. Decades of struggling for financial success and security have taught the Jewish woman a great deal about what it means to survive. And apparently survival means something completely different than it does in the dictionary; survival is accomplishment. What Mollie Parnis, Elizabeth Holtzman and even some of their more materially-oriented sisters have learned is the same lesson: use what you have, your talents and strengths, to get exactly what you want.

If the legacy of the past reflects the struggle to achieve against overwhelming odds often at great sacrifice, what will become of the future generation of Jewish Princesses who may not know from struggles and sacrifices at all? How much inherited strength will be retained by children brought up in today's wall-to-wall carpeted world?

The answer may not be completely clear at present. Most brand-new Jewish Princesses are too small to demonstrate how their gilded infancies will affect their personalities. And yet I would caution anyone from being misled by today's solid-gold childhoods, because it is a safe bet that Jewish children will still have a good deal of strength to tap in their lifetimes. As we have seen, a desire to achieve runs in the blood and Jewish pampering also includes a good deal of success-oriented nudging.

Certainly, it is lucky for the Jewish Princess that coddling does not affect her inner drive. Because no baby has been as worshiped as the little Jewish Princess (or Prince). The arrival of a new baby is the acknowledged signal to begin the whole cycle of spoiling over again, complete with all updated, modern extras. Because, career success aside, the next star-studded extravaganza in the life of the Jewish Princess is the birth of her baby.

9

"BE FRUITFUL AND MULTIPLY"

It is hard to raise sons; and much harder to raise daughters.

—Sholom Aleichem

When a Jewish Princess has a baby, assuredly she does not go it alone. Her mother and father do everything short of having it for her. The classic story—Helene Gershman recalls when she was pregnant and living in Boston with her doctor-husband. Her parents, who lived in New York City, waited anxiously at home for the phone call that their daughter's labor had begun. No matter how far away Jewish parents are, they must Be There when the baby finally arrives. One night, the pains began and Helene's husband, dutiful son-in-law, called the folks long distance. "Now," he told them, "I'll be taking Helene to the hospital very soon."

Grabbing coats and bags, the excited parents ran into a waiting cab. "La Guardia Airport and hurry," they told the driver. "Our daughter is having her baby!" They landed via shuttle at Logan Airport, where another cab ferried them to the hospital. Running into the main lobby, they found the admissions desk and asked for their daughter. The nurse checked the records, then looked up and informed them crisply, "We have no one admitted here by that name." They had made it to the hospital before their daughter did.

Such feats are commonplace among Jewish grandparents. A nurse at one Long Island hospital sourly recalls chasing the new grandmothers out from behind curtains and inside closets after visiting hours at the maternity floor ended. Guests at a fashionable cocktail party might be exposed to the endless harangue of a newly blessed grandma as the highlight of the evening. One such woman produced a small cassette tape player at a recent gathering. "My grandchild," she said proudly, and turned on the tape. The guests, who expected at least a singsong version of "Mary Had a Little Lamb," instead heard gurglings, cooing, babbling and sounds of spitting up, amplified to a high degree.

Where does all of this nutsy behavior begin? As soon as the rabbit tests or urine specimen reports are in. At that moment, the baby is a *fait accompli*. A positive pregnancy report sets off a chain of activity and concern the likes of which many children after birth never see.

But how, you ask, is an unborn baby pampered? Easy. Through the mother. The pregnant Jewish Princess is treated like a Queen, throughout what can only be described as nine months of sheer bliss. Is it any wonder, then, that she has developed ways to accommodate her feelings and not waste a single, glorious moment? The official word from the gynecologist ("Well, we've got some happy news here, little mother") triggers a barrage of phone calls. She tells Everyone, Immediately. "Guess what! I'm two weeks pregnant!"

Without even the slightest perceptible bulge showing in her tummy, she runs out to buy maternity clothes in order to have things to climb into the minute she thinks she's going to show. Jewish Princess Pregnancy Chic is almost as important as pregnancy itself. And pregnancy is also the time to make those kvetches count, ladies. But be careful. Too much complaining results in Mother descending on your head, so it must be handled very delicately.

A Jewish Princess says, "I found myself describing my conditions and symptoms to everyone, every day. Nothing really bothered me too much, I was nauseous and all, but I liked letting everyone know how I was feeling." News bulletins go something like this: "Hello, Ma? Why did it take me so long to answer the phone? Because I was throwing up in the bathroom. No, I'm really fine. No, don't come over. A nice cup of tea? Mother, you're gonna make me throw up again."

A pregnant Jewish Princess needs catering to, pampering and humoring. "Give in to her," the husband and parents say, and down through the ages, generations of Jewish families have done just that, with special rules applying. Don't go to funerals, don't look at crippled people on the street, don't collect baby things.

Why all the attention? Because the Jewish Princess is with child, and "mit kinder" a marriage becomes truly blessed, a fulfillment of God's commandment to "be fruitful and multiply."

Today, being fruitful opens the princess to the question, to suffer or not to suffer? The great natural childbirth versus anesthesia debate. The Jewish Princess who sampled the more painful Lamaze way reported back, "I'll never do it again." How come? "It hurts too much." A fair assessment, and since the princess is not a natural-born sufferer, the choice often becomes much simpler. Nudged by her mother, "So whaddya want to suffer any more than you have to? Believe me, you'll go through plenty anyhow," many princesses settle on a combination of both. She takes the classes, dragging her husband along for the full panting preparations, and then, at the moment of truth, she settles for a spinal. And, as one satisfied customer said, "It was like having a tooth out."

At about the same time, the parents-to-be start with the Name-the-Baby routine. They sit up, for months, with their lists. After all, no future Jewish Prince or Princess should be stuck with a plain, uninteresting name. As a result, the daughter of a Susan is rarely, say, a Barbara. A daughter should have a different, special name. The result? Today all of the Nancys and Lindas and Janes are dishing out fancy, multisyllabled Christian debutante names, coupling them with the homey, latkes-heavy Jewish last names.

A sample set of names follows, culled from some baby announcements I received during the past year. Choose one from Column A and one from Column B.

A	B
Candice Melissa	Schwartz
Melinda Cheryll	Appelbaum
Jocelyn Amy	Horowitz
Alyssa Diane	Finklestein
Amanda Carolyn	Kleinberg
Traci Dawn	Guggenheimer
Erica Lauren	Seligstein
Robyn Allison	Teitelbaum
Sacha Margo	Katzman

Traditionally, the selection of names for Jewish children was purposeful and limited. But where are the Sadies and Raizels of yesteryear? The first initials of the names may still be used in honor of a beloved, deceased relative the family wishes to honor, but the new names are a long way from the Bible or the shtetl.

Another recent naming trend has taken ethnic-conscious mothers back to their roots, but sometimes the return is only a part-way trip, resulting in a clashing of two cultures: Sarah Nicole! Rachel Kerrie! In other families, the birth announcements read as though parents were suffering an attack of the Jewish guilts in the midst of their child-naming years. Marc and Candy (née Kohn) Rabinowitz's first two daughters were called Danielle Alexandra and Stephanie Deena. Then a change occurs. The third kid winds up with the name of Esther Leah.

One final princess tactic, aimed at giving daughter the

Unique moniker, is to change the spelling of a more
ordinary name in favor of something a bit more
continental. (These names seem to have been dreamed up
by the folks who brought you LaVine from Levine.) The
tricks of the trade are doubled consonants, dropped *y*'s for
i's, and twinned *e*'s. A simple name, such as Cheryl, can
become exotic: try Cheryll. Or a nicknamed version,
Cheri, Sherry, Cherree. The ultimate variation? Sherrill.
One wealthy, social family one-upped the competition
years ago when they named their daughter Cheray.

The results of this new naming trend can astonish even
those mothers who have followed its dictates. Ellen Bayer,
a Manhattan woman in her early thirties, recalled the
culture shock she underwent while dropping her three-
year-old daughter at a pre-school exercise class held at the
Ninety-second Street YMHA. She walked into the
classroom, chock-full of well-dressed little East and West
Side princesses, ready for tumbling in their tiny Danskins.
"I listened as the teacher began to call the class to order
and it struck me that the names of these kids were all
unreal. My own daughter Jennifer was playing with a
bunch of little Jewish girls who answered to the names of
Nicole, Alyssa and Samantha. Two years later, when I had
a son, I named him Shimon Moshe. And now my daughter
has learned to identify herself by her English and Hebrew
names. She's Jenny and Zahava."

Certainly Jenny-or-Zahava Bayer has something more
in common with those other little exercising princesses at
the "Y" than merely her first name. She came into the

166

world, just as they did, in an atmosphere of joyous celebration. Next to the Jewish wedding the birth of a baby is the ultimate moment of kvelling. In a Massachusetts hospital, one gentile mother reported in great awe that the princess in the next room had a crowd of people around her from early morning until late at night. A friendly group, they occasionally looked in next door, and when they discovered the non-Jewish woman was visited only by her husband, "They looked at me as though I were an orphan."

The fervor reaches its highest pitch when the princess goes into labor. Linda Meyerson schleps up the steps of Mount Sinai Hospital in New York City, panting, followed by her retinue: the husband with a canvas suitcase, her father carrying copies of the latest best-sellers and a Dr. Spock in paperback, and the soon-to-be-a-grandmother holding a "leaving-the-hospital dress" in a plastic dry cleaning bag and Linda's Carmen electric curlers. Inside the overnight bag is a matching nightgown and bathrobe that her mother has thoughtfully bought as a last minute gift, after she discovered Linda was going to wear her old flannel number postpartum. "You can't do that," Mother shrieked, and was off in a flash with her charge plate. Linda should only know from her mother's days, when she herself was born. No self-respecting Jewish Princess in the 1940's went into the hospital with anything less than a handmade, monogrammed peignoir set, a lacy bed jacket, and a satin blanket cover, designed to be thrown over those tacky hospital sheets. Linda checks in with her store-bought John Kloss outfit. Then the princess departs for the labor room and the wait begins. The grandparents arrive and two sets of elder parents sit nervously with one Jewish Prince, waiting for the news. Fourteen hours later, word comes down: Linda has had a girl. "Great, marvelous," they chorus. Linda's father, tears in his eyes, looks at his son-in-law, puts his arm around his shoulders and says, "Come, let's go for a walk." They stroll arm in arm down past the soda and cigarette machines and stop in a quiet corner. The new grandfather then gives his son-in-law The Talk. "I just want to tell you something I found out from experience. I hope you're not disappointed it wasn't a boy. But let me tell you, this is the luckiest thing to happen to you. I have daughters, and they are security for the future. You'll always have your daughter. And let me also say, your baby was smart to be born a girl." Perhaps in this little tale, the grandpa showed how he really had missed having a son, but no matter. While the men philosophized, the mothers were joyous. They know what great fun it is to raise a Jewish Princess. "Samantha Lyn Meyerson," they pronounce in the hospital lobby. They are not crying because it's a girl.

After the long night vigil, it is already morning and soon time for visiting hours. The husband, however, is allowed a peek before the official time begins and he reports back to this battle station after his quick visit. "She looks terrific," he tells the folks about Linda. Anyone had better believe Linda looks terrific. After her night with the obstetrician, she spent the morning on the telephone, simultaneously applying blush-on and her false eyelashes, and then kept a date with the hospital beautician. Her hair done, she waited propped up in bed, to Receive. Mother, fresh from the phone booth and emptied of the roll of dimes she brought along for calls, arrived first, at the head of the shopping bag cadre who visit the maternity floor daily. Rushing out of the elevator come a host of store names flashing on paper wrappers, Godiva, Zabar's, Bloomingdale's, crunching and crackling their way into the rooms. "Linda!" shouts Mother, who rushes over and plants kisses in the air, God forbid she should mess up her makeup. "Daddy will be up in a minute, he can't find a parking place." Mother moves the floral arrangements to one side, and starts to unpack. Out of her bags come jars of macadamia nuts, boxes of stuffed dates, two bottles of J&B, one of Jack Daniels, and a set of paper cups and matching cocktail napkins (printed with tiny infants riding in World War I-vintage planes and waving). Linda's friends begin to file into the room now, all with some small gift in hand, a baby present or a hospital room object, candy, flowers, perfume, powder, and cunning baby cards. Hors d'oeuvres are passed, and the friends' husbands drift into the halls to discuss last night's Knicks game.

The babies are on view behind the glass window and the grandparents of Linda's little girl join the crush. They indulge in that traditional exercise in comparative anatomy that invokes the old "knock on wood" form of expression. "Thank God she doesn't have Milton's nose," says paternal grandma. "Kineahora, such a gorgeous

169

baby," says maternal grandma in response. Early claims are laid for family side of the chin, ears, size of hands and feet and shape of mouth. Over to one corner, an aunt of Linda's recalled her son's birth, as the sounds of praise ring through the halls. "Everyone was just raving about him, and he was probably the ugliest baby I'd ever seen. Long feet and hands, and all of this flesh hanging from his arms and a squashed-looking face. Then they brought my grandmother over to see him. She stood and stared at that child, then turned around, and told everyone, 'Look. He has such beautiful fixtures!' "

By the time Samantha Lyn Meyerson is twenty-four hours old, she has received: a custom-made English baby carriage, a crib with an attached musical fish mobile, a lacy Saks Fifth Avenue layette, and six lines of small type in the New York *Times* baby announcements column, to run the following Sunday. Mother Linda Meyerson has made a small haul of her own, including a special prize from her best friend, six weeks of exercise classes at the Jack LaLanne in her neighborhood.

And lest the family worry that Linda might knock herself out, have no fear. A baby nurse has been hired for a month, to take charge of momma and daughter until Linda can take over. Plus, of course, requisite help from Momma who has purchased a second crib and playpen for the guest room in her White Plains home.

Linda Meyerson, like many other young women of her generation, will be able to do for Samantha everything her mother did for her, but at no sacrifice. Linda tends to deemphasize the importance of spending money because she has not gone through a terrible struggle to obtain it. Today, the parents substitute another cause célèbre: They set limits. Linda and her husband talk philosophically about not spending too much on their baby. "I want Samantha to know about good things," Linda said. "She'll probably have a great deal. I can't stop my mother and mother-in-law from buying stuff, but I intend to set certain limits." Gone is the intense fight of previous generations to make life for the child measurably better. Life is better to begin with, these days.

And if, in these relatively prosperous times, there is any doubt about the future of the Jewish Princess, forget it. We can safely predict that another generation of Jewish Princesses, and Princes, is on the way. If children, once upon a time, represented a Jewish family's step up the economic and social ladder, today they reflect the maintenance of a particular life-style. What you cannot do without for yourself, you certainly cannot skip for the kinder.

Listen to the stockbroker in his Pierre Cardin suit, Gucci loafers and Turnbull & Asser tie, shaking his head over the influx of Bonwit Teller bills following the birth of his new daughter. "I can't understand my wife," he said, perplexed. "She spends eight hundred dollars on the baby's clothes, which the kid will outgrow in five minutes. She has to buy everything in the most expensive stores. I haven't got a cent left over to buy any clothes for myself this year!"

Or watch the mother in Cerutti, a very posh, very expensive, high-status children's clothing boutique on Madison Avenue in New York. She selects a hand-embroidered, tiny denim pants outfit for her daughter. What's the play suit for? "She'll wear this when she goes to the park," the mother says, with an expression on her face indicating, but of course, for the park. The outfit costs close to fifty dollars. I tell her I think the price is a little high. She shrugs. "I spend this much because I want my daughter to start out knowing what the good things are."

Jewish mothers of infants and very small children are not unaware of the result of their high-minded purchases and consistent spending. They know they are producing a generation which could conceivably out-princess any previous group of girls. But with no hesitation, they tell tales of precocious taste and pampering the same way other mothers report on bowel movements and jigsaw puzzle prowess.

In an apartment in Fort Lee, New Jersey, a small group of young mommas has gathered to discuss some of their attitudes toward motherhood. They agree to use only their first names because they do not want to involve their unseen husbands, so I refer to them as Nancy, Marilyn, and Karen. They are in their late twenties to early thirties and have children ranging in age from five months to five years. Their husbands are businessmen, with middle to upper middle-class incomes. Apparently, the women are not afraid to spend money freely, as their clothes, jewelry and hair styles indicate. Fresh from beauty parlors, their combed locks gleam in the overhead light and their diamond rings twinkle together in a glassy ensemble.

We are sitting in Marilyn's den, a wood-paneled room recently decorated in Scandinavian modern. A bright Rya rug sits on the floor, in purple and red tones, a long couch is covered with groupings of embroidered crewel pillows, and a wall unit of shelves faces the couch on the opposite side. Marilyn sits by a window, in a leather chair, with her feet on a matching ottoman. Nancy sits nearby on a club chair, while Karen, who is nervous and less talkative, perches on the couch, gets up and walks around, and eventually leaves early.

Before we started to talk, I found myself staring at that wall unit. There were not many books on the shelves, a few best-sellers, a handful of paperbacks, but there were some interesting chotchkes. High on the top shelf, facing the room, two things caught my eye. There was a modern, sterling silver menorah, polished and gleaming, set off to one side of a shelf, while at the other end, distinctly paired with the religious candelabra, was a silver-framed portrait of Marilyn's little boy, apparently taken in a department store, seated on Santa Claus' lap. The sight gives me pause.

I first asked the three ladies if they thought they themselves were spoiled. They nodded. "Yes," said Marilyn, dark-haired and dark-eyed. "Our husbands spoil us. If you want something, you buy it."

"Do you think your children are spoiled?" I asked.

Again, I get a unanimous response. "Absolutely yes," Nancy said. Nancy is petite, with a short, light brown shag haircut. "But I think we'd all agree we want to give our children good values."

173

We discuss what values they mean. Education comes up first. Nancy pointed out that everyone's kids go to private schools, or will go as soon as they are old enough. Progressive nursery school education is one value.

Toys? "There isn't a toy in the world my husband and I can find to buy my son and daughter anymore," Marilyn said. "Their playroom looks like F.A.O. Schwarz. But they don't realize they're different in that way from anyone else. Their friends all have the same things."

Karen, blond and pouting, finally seemed to come alive. She nodded her head, and said, "Our children associate with kids who have the same life-style." Then she lapsed back into her sultry coma.

Marilyn began to get more excited about the subject. "Look," she said, shifting her position on the chair and leaning forward, "if you buy them an extra toy, it won't kill them. My little boy likes to go on vacations. But yours"—and with this she turned to Nancy, faintly but humorously accusing—"your kids want to go to Palm Beach every day."

Nancy did not seem to think the remark was very funny. Marilyn continued to chatter on. "I truly believe that our children don't have to have the best toys or clothes, as long as they look neat and nice and have a few good things. But there's always the temptation to do too much." She sighed.

All of the women employ full-time household help. But not one would consider taking a job at this time because their children are "too young." They make themselves available, with a vengeance, to do things with the children. Marilyn proudly noted that she still has a baby nurse for her five-month-old daughter because she did not want her small son to feel neglected. The women believe that their presence in the home and their rigorous participation in their children's lives is essential.

Daily schedules feature schleps to the zoo, cartoon shows, the park, the ice skating rink, and friends' homes. In addition, there are seasonal trips to Florida to visit the grandparents. The ladies are involved in organizing a Saturday play group for special forays into Manhattan. And, lest the children find their apartment or home life indoors a bore, they can all retire to specially-built playrooms, such as the one in Marilyn's fourth bedroom, which features a yellow and red mini jungle gym, shelves of toys and games, a tiny Panasonic TV set, a blackboard, and two easels.

Whenever possible, the mommies include the kiddies on a few choice excursions to the cream of New York department stores, to designer showrooms, shops and boutiques, to the Autopub for lunch, and to Tiffany's. Whatever happened to Macy's toy department? I thought. Aloud, I asked them what they thought the effect of the adults' "good life" was on the wee ones?

Amusing, at times, the mothers agreed. The child's eye view was certainly refreshing. Nancy contributed one item. "My four-year-old daughter knows the names of all the jewels in Van Cleef & Arpels' windows. I don't know what they're teaching them in nursery school these days," she noted with some chagrin.

Karen, startled into reacting again, drawled, "That's nothing. My kid went with me to a jewelry auction at

Parke-Bernet. All the way up in the elevator, she was singing over and over, 'I'm going to see the diamonds and the rubies.'"

The mothers again agreed that all of this "spoiling" was not their idea alone. Their husbands condoned it, and their parents were full-time sponsors as well. Nancy's four-year-old was going to see Europe in a few months with her grandma and grandpa at her side. "They're going to go to London first, and they'll stay at Claridge's," she noted with great pride. Only the best hotel in town is suitable for a Jewish Princess, even though her throne is still but a mere high chair.

Suddenly, there were sounds of a small scuffle and the children in question tumbled into the room. Marilyn's oldest boy, five, was running away from Nancy's girls, the four-year-old and her two-and-a-half-year-old baby sister. The royal darlings look the same as just about any neatly dressed children from the New York metropolitan area. Spoiled, perhaps, but in front of company they are shy. They sit on the floor and push around model trucks. Marilyn immediately noticed that her son was wiping his nose; glancing at her Lucite watch, she said it was time to take him to the doctor for his weekly allergy shots.

We bundled into coats and walked out to the elevator. As we traveled down to the lobby, I overheard Marilyn talking to Nancy about a birthday cake she planned to buy, for eighteen dollars. Eighteen dollars for a cake? I asked myself. Her little boy also heard the conversation, and he tugged at the hem of his mother's fur coat. "For me?" he said. "Yes," she answered with an isn't-that-wonderful smile. The small boy turned and said excitedly to Nancy's older daughter, "Maybe it'll be like last year's." What was last year? I asked him. "A real garage," he whooped. "With real cars and trucks on it." Can you top that this year, William Greenberg bakers?

Do these women represent just a small portion of the contemporary Jewish mothers of America? Probably yes, but they serve to prove a point. Even women who say they are not interested in gross materialism express similar attitudes toward their offspring. One mother said she conscientiously avoided dressing up her little girls "like dolls" and spent time reading to them instead, then added with a small sigh that she felt she had missed something. "I always wish I got more pleasure out of the dressing-up aspect. Too bad I really hate to shop." And in the home of one full-time working momma, where the children are left to a housekeeper's care, the mother fights with her own impulses in order to limit the amount she buys for her kids. "I have to be careful *not* to give my kids everything I want to give them. That takes a lot of hard work." Years ago, parents worked hard to provide everything, today they work hard not to give too much.

Still, there is more to the Jewish Princess story than ending with the girl in the golden palace raising a couple of pampered progeny. For the princess has more to give than merely material things. What she will pass on to the next generation of Jewish Princesses and Princes is affection, warmth, love and a good deal of self-awareness. A small surprise for the future is in store: the Jewish Princess can be all Jewish and liberated and a very healthy influence on her family as well. Take heart. It is time for Jewish Princess Liberation.

10

POWER TO THE PRINCESS

> She openeth her mouth with wisdom.
> —The Jewish "Woman of Valor," Proverbs

The idea of a liberated Jewish Princess would seem to be a contradiction in terms. After all, no liberated woman is going to stand in the kitchen for three hours making homemade chicken soup with matzo balls. And, conversely, no real Jewish mother would be caught dead letting her linoleum floors get all scuffed while she's out stuffing envelopes for the cause, right?

Wrong. A number of pop psychologists will tell you that the Jewish Princess comes from a long line of originally liberated females. Even with all of the mikva nonsense and banishment to the balcony of the synagogue, Jewish women still took on many financial and business responsibilities in order that their husbands might be free to discuss Talmud daily. And here in America, strict religious sexism has waned while a new cult of Jewish female appreciation has flowered. Thus, the Jewish-American woman can possess the self-confidence, education and training to adjust to a new liberated role even more smoothly than her shiksa sisters.

Today's liberated Jewish Princess is Golda Meir with an all-electric kitchen and a Haitian housekeeper; she is Emma Goldman with a charge account at Bloomingdale's. The mixture of "Right On" with haimish is no problem for the princess.

Barbara Seaman is a modern Jewish momma who combines career, motherhood and feminism with ease. I waited for her, late from an appointment at Georgette Klinger's Skin Care Salon, in her Manhattan, West Side apartment, located in the heart of the good old Jewish half-mile turf. Barbara is the author of one of the classic women's liberation books of the last decade, *Free and Female.*

The Seaman residence is doctor's office for Dr. Seaman, Barbara's psychiatrist husband, and home for the family. Shira, Barbara's twelve-year-old daugher, a dark-haired child in jeans, opened the door for me. She is a Hunter High School seventh grader who was in the midst of planning a Halloween bash with a friend. She showed me into the kitchen, to wait.

I could not wait to see what the feminist's kitchen was like, how different it would be from those unliberated, non-Movement kitchens with which I had become familiar. It isn't very different. The cabinets are brown wood, the refrigerator is a burnished copper color, there is a round table and group of chairs in a corner under a wagon-wheel chandelier and a sideboard with shelves next to it. Over by the telephone is a cork bulletin board embellished with memos and political buttons. The kitchen is comfortably cluttered, a box of Veri-Thin Pretzels out on a counter, cans of Fresca and Tab on the table, piles of doctors' magazines and books on a chair. On the sideboard shelves are cookbooks. *The Art of Jewish Cooking* by Jennie Grossinger catches my eye, and a small stack of books on the subject of abortion. Tsimis and tsuris on the space of one shelf, I thought as the front door opened and in marched a youthful figure in slouch hat of plaid wool, fur-collared rust-red sweater and jeans, clutching a Georgette Klinger paper bag of facial goodies. "Hello, so sorry to keep you waiting," she said with a big, friendly smile. Klinger goodies deposited on the table, she reached for a cold drink. Did I want some? No? Shall we go into the bedroom to talk? Fine.

Her skin looks terrific, Klinger and all. She glows, from the care and the cold, and her hair is cut short, ruffled, light brown with blond streaks. She is not really describable in a word, neither sylphlike nor stocky nor plain nor gorgeous, but there is a certain quality. I settle on warm. At thirty-nine, she has an open face, with eager, wide eyes, a nice figure and a casual, homey look. With her jeans she wore a printed green shirt, and hanging from her neck on chains, a watch and a twisted, gold women's liberation symbol.

The bedroom is enormous, with a double bed covered with a blue spread, piles of pillows at the head, a wooden console with TV on one wall, a white mantel and fireplace facing the bed, a Victorian-style couch and a coffee table in one corner and an office desk and swivel chair against the wall opposite the television. A light Oriental rug covers the floor and on the walls are yards of gold printed wallpaper, quite faded and worn in spots.

Barbara kicked off her shoes and planted herself on the bed next to the phone. Grabbing an ashtray (she chain-smokes fiercely), she lit the first of her dozen or more cigarettes and started with a definition of Jewish Princess, at my request.

"I've been asking people what they think the term means. I have this friend, a newspaper reporter who's an Indiana Methodist. She told me she really knows about the Jewish Princess because she works for the New York *Post*. To her, the term refers to one essential quality, chutzpah. But I think what she really means isn't chutzpah. That's not quite the right word. It's more hubris, assuming you can get what you want. A girl who feels that because she's there, good things should be happening to her."

Barbara's research on the subject included asking her husband for a definition, too. She reported his answer as suffused with a neat, psychiatric logic: "She is someone who expects men to be very, very nice to her, her father, her husband, her sons, her brothers." Heigh-ho, Freud, I thought.

I asked Barbara whether anything was changing for young Jewish women in light of women's liberation. Ms. Seaman noted that a study of the influence of Jewish mothers on their daughters indicated that many young women have vowed not to allow themselves to invest too much in their own children. "They do not want to feel that life is over when their children grow up and leave home.

After seeing their mothers experience that kind of depression, these young women express a desire to change their roles."

The phone rang. Barbara quickly answered, telling the caller that she was in the midst of an interview. Then she reacted excitedly to the news that this friend had apparently found an apartment on the West Side. Barbara crowed, "Welcome to Zabar Country." Then, considerately, hung up and turned her attention back to the interview.

Since Barbara's next book is on motherhood, she had a bit of advance research to contribute to our talk. "I'm gathering that what's happening with young women is, generally, they've made a lot of resolutions ahead of time, that to be totally involved with their children is not healthy. They just don't want to be too absorbed with motherhood alone." Then she sat bolt upright on the bed, and crossed her legs for added emphasis. "But," she said, "when they actually have their first child, it seems as though it is hard for them to be different from their mothers."

"But aren't there some real changes to be seen among young Jewish women?" I probed, certain that Barbara's involvement with feminism must have shown her some observable differences.

"Oh, yes," she answered. "Jewish women are really getting it together. Women today, for example, can say more frequently, if my daughter wants to be a doctor, that's really wonderful, God bless her."

Yet Ms. Seaman was quick to point out a few major Jewish hang-ups. In her opinion, the Jewish religion is fraught with "misogyny, worse than Christianity because at least they have a few prominent female figures, like Mary." She also believes that strength among Jewish women might be seen as a negative attribute, a reaction to oppression: "I think any strength they had came from hearing their grandfathers pray every day, thanking God they were not women."

These remarks prompted me to ask her about her own upbringing, because Barbara Seaman is no downtrodden little Jewish baleboosteh. Where did she get her strength from, I asked, and is it possible to be a feminist Jewish Princess?

According to Barbara, it is. "I'm really a deviant Jewish Princess," she said. How deviant? "To begin with, my parents thought clothes were a terrible waste of money. We were not raised as angora-sweater types. And we never lived on West End Avenue when we were growing up, only on side streets. Today, my sister and I both live on West End and she says maybe we always really wanted to. My father, now he's really arrived. He lives on Central Park West, in the El Dorado."

Barbara Seaman is, by her own admission, a strange combination of Jewish Princess and liberated woman. "Today I spend too much on clothes, of course. Want to see the designer labels in my closet? It takes a lot of effort to spend as much as I do and look like a slob. Look, I live on the West Side, I'm a writer and a feminist, but see?" With this, she stood up, picked up a pair of green suede shoes off the floor, and brought them over to me, pointing to the inner lining. "Givenchy, right? And this shirt?" She bent her head down and plucked the back collar of her green blouse off her neck so I could read the label. It said "Elizabeth Arden." And just returned from Klinger as well. Ah-hah, a closet Jewish Princess!

Barbara's elder daughter Elana then entered the room, a fourteen-year-old who does not really care much about clothes from good stores. She is dressed in ninth grade fashion, a T-shirt and jeans, her long hair hangs down around her round face. With her circular eyeglasses and intense, serious look on her face, she appears pensive and wise. Barbara is quite proud of her. Elana is currently creating a women's curriculum of her own at her private school, a project she initiated when she discovered few courses had enough information on women. Elana is Barbara's junior alter ego in the family.

"I want you to tell her about Jewish Princesses," Barbara said to her daughter.

Solemn Elana looked thoughtful, then replied, "I didn't hear about them until my mother asked me a few days ago." Her brother Noah, seventeen, walked in on that remark and snorted, saying, "Of course you know them at school."

"Noah knows dozens," Barbara said. "He goes to Dalton."

While Elana and Noah argued about who knew what, Shira came into the room, crawled onto the bed, put her head on her mother's shoulder and gave her a big hug.

I went on. "Do young women your age concentrate more on their wardrobes or on college and their future professions?" I asked Elana.

185

"Both," she said, then added, "It depends on their personalities. But I think more of them think about college."

"Hah," said Noah, the family princess-maven. "That's because they already have the wardrobe."

By now, I gathered that this show of family en masse meant more than a devouring interest in the subject of Jewish Princesses. Supper was on and they were waiting for Mommy. Then, Dr. Seaman walked in.

Barbara made it a family affair by asking her husband, "Why do you daddies spend all that money on your little girls, buying them nice things?"

Dr. Seaman, a kindly-looking man with a yeshiva bucher beard, tossed off an answer on his way in to eat. "It makes him feel loved."

Dinner was a quick meal, chicken, lima beans, coleslaw, milk and a pitcher of iced tea, served in the kitchen, with everyone anxious to get back to what he was doing. The kids had homework, Dr. Seaman had his couch and patients, and Barbara and I the interview. Glasses of iced tea in hand, we returned to the bedroom to finish up the final questions on the Jewish Princess Facing Life.

But before we continued more general social observations, Ms. Seaman told me some of her own problems as a verbal, active, outspoken feminist. A lot of people seem to find her super-militant, she said, and noted that one writer recently called her *la furiosa* after a college speaking engagement. Barbara is genuinely perplexed and rather hurt by such remarks. "I don't understand that reaction. My statements are not hostile. But I'm seen as a real militant feminist."

Curious as to whether this is Barbara's problem alone, I asked her about other Jewish feminists. Maybe Jewish women, used to being loved creatures at home, are hurt at not being loved in public?

"One thing about the Jewish feminists in my circle of friends, writers in New York, is their public image of being so strong. We get heckled. A friend of mine is so brave in public, so very tough." But the impression Barbara gave was that no one was all that thick-skinned in reality. Her friends had good marriages, loving husbands, children who were obedient and respectful, but publicly some were perceived as terrors.

A Jewish feminist needs backbone. If you're Barbara Seaman, none of it came from pampering. "I feel like a waif, the opposite thing from being a princess," she said, referring to her unpampered, un-angora-sweatered childhood. But always there was faith in her abilities. "Of course," she said, pointing to a dedication she had written in one of her books, "I thanked my father for his unfailing confidence in me. For me, and my sisters, who are gifted artists and not as ambitious and aggressive as I am, our father always had faith. He felt we could do no wrong. You got a bad grade, he would say, something must be wrong with the teacher!"

What Barbara gives her children is the same "unfailing confidence" her father had in her. She dotes on her kids' brightness, their achievements, their wishes for themselves. She spent a few minutes during our talk discussing Noah's screen-writing ambitions. And when he wandered into the room (the door was always left open), she praised his work in a writing course at school. "Oh, Ma," he pshawed, saying the teacher didn't know. "The teacher thinks you're really good," she told him firmly. If part of being a princess or prince is being believed in, the Seaman kids have got it in spades.

But for the last word on the children, I asked Elana outright if she thought she was valued by her parents. She replied, "Sometimes they do make me feel that way, sometimes they don't, but most of the time they do. They do more than most people do." She looked at her mother, who smiled at her, waiting to hear her full reply. Elana gestured at her mother. "Sometimes she doesn't listen, she goes 'Un Hunnh, Un Hunnh'!"

"That's when I'm writing," Barbara said.

"But you're not typing," her daughter shot back.

"Yes, but I'm writing in my head," she countered, turning toward me for support. "You know, you don't have to be typing to be working on something."

But Elana did admit she was a "loved, beloved child." "Yes," she said, simply and solemnly, those round glasses emphasizing her serious eyes.

I ended the interview by asking Ms. Seaman if she thought she was a Jewish Princess.

"I asked my husband that one," she said. His answer? "I'm an unconventional one, he said. A lot of women are straight down the line Jewish Princesses, but I think I'm a deviant one."

And then the Seaman women marched out ensemble to have cones at Baskin-Robbins. Everyone, that is, except Elana. Serious as ever, she was taking this night, erev Yom Kippur, to begin her first fast, "not because I'm terribly

Jewish but because I've never really known how hunger feels, what so many people go through all the time." Fasting means no Rocky Road, and so, abstemious, she forgoes a cone for principle.

What does the Seaman experience offer us? A view of the future as Now, perhaps. A working, feminist, albeit Jewish Princess mother, raising three children, with the requisite doctor-husband, the enormous (though not lavish) apartment and a terrific housekeeper to provide an assist. Barbara's strengths are her own, her work is quite time-consuming, yet she has given her family an apparent abundance of love and warmth. And catering. Noah needed a phone number? His mother read it to him. "Ah, Ma," he said." "I can't remember it." "You want me to write it down?" she asked. "Yeah," he said, standing there helplessly. She did, without a murmur. Nice Mommy, I thought.

"Oh, we have our problems," Barbara said at one point with a wry twist of a smile, but who doesn't have problems? Still, she has the Jewish Princess capability and confidence. And her household exudes that haimish sit-right-down-and-join-the-family glow of many of the other Jewish homes I visited.

Years and years ago, when the Jews lived crowded on the shtetls of Russian and Eastern Europe, families used to say, "If you have daughters, you have no use for laughter." No poor family laughed when they had to sell furniture to provide a dowry, sign up with a shadchen and pay a fee to land her a husband, or make a wedding to which the entire village had to be invited, en masse. Who could laugh when a child was born who would neither study Torah nor learn Hebrew, who could not inherit the business or say Kaddish over your grave and insure the trip to heaven?

None of that chozzerai holds much water anymore. Parents are genuinely delighted with their girls. And they have plenty of use for laughter; for they do in fact smile all the way to the bank (to make the requisite withdrawals).

Certainly, the term Jewish Princess has a negative connotation. But isn't it about time that we got it into our heads that being a Jewish Princess is something she, and we, can be proud of? She represents generations of achievement, years of industry, and training, a lifetime of indulgence and hard work. It is not easy to be a Jewish Princess.

In accepting what she is and who she is, the Jewish Princess gains strength to persevere. And whether she achieves her goals or not, no one can ever convince her she has failed. She has survived in great style over the years, unbowed by fluctuations in the Dow Jones, in spite of a Depression and a few wars. Now we are at the glorious moment in the princess' history when much of her expectation has been fulfilled. Now, we think, she can relax at last, secure in the knowledge that everything is the way she wants it to be.

But for a Jewish Princess, there is no seventh day on which to rest. Part of the great fun of watching the princess is her constant motion, her never-ending flood of ideas, plans, preparations, and assigned tasks.

And at a time when clothes, advertising, entertainment and the like have become stylized and possess a stultifying conformity, the Jewish Princess remains curiously aber- rant. Though she may follow current trends, she remains faithful to her parents in an age of family discord, nudgy with her children at a time when such things are supposed to be kept cool, free with her opinions and advice when most people want to talk to experts, and in total, just as hard to please and as fussy as though she were the incarnation of her smart, sly old baleboosteh great-grand- ma. The strong Jewish lady of the past and the smart, dedicated woman of the future are contained within the persona of one pleasant, attractive, sharp young woman, the Jewish Princess. And in anyone's lifetime, she is not to be missed.